C000066787

BOSS'S SECRET BABY

A SECOND CHANCE ROMANCE

CRYSTAL MONROE

"I never forgot you, Isabelle. I won't stop until you're screaming my name again."

Five years ago, Carter was my everything... for one night.
I fell for Mr. Perfect hours before he left town.
Since then, I live on memories of his rock-hard body.

Until I see my new boss.
The moment Carter's intense blue eyes meet mine, I freeze.
This time, he's not letting me slip through his fingers.
There's no escape from his panty-melting grin...
Or the dirty talk he whispers in my ear.

But Carter's not the only one with surprises.
I've kept a big secret all these years.
Our sweet little boy with Carter's blue eyes.

Can our second chance survive a secret this big?

Copyright © 2021 by Crystal Monroe

All rights reserved.

No part of this book may be reproduced in any form or by any electronic or mechanical means, including information storage and retrieval systems, without written permission from the author, except for the use of brief quotations in a book review.

CHAPTER 1

ISABELLE

Five Years Ago

"*A*re you kidding me?" I cried out, staring at Ryan.

He sat back in his chair, nonchalant as hell, looking like he hadn't just ripped my whole world apart.

"Come on, babe. It's better this way."

I shook my head. I couldn't wrap my mind around the fact that Ryan had taken me out on a date night just to break up with me. Who arranges a break-up date?

"How is it better?" I asked, trying not to let my voice tremble or to sound like I was going to cry. Which was exactly what I felt like doing. "We've been together for two years, and you're just throwing it all away."

"I'm not throwing it all away, babe." He leaned forward, reaching for my hand over the table.

"*Don't* call me that," I said, snatching my hand away before he could touch me. "You're dumping me. You can go right back to using my name."

"Fine, *Isabelle*," Ryan said, making my name sound like it

1

tasted bad in his mouth. "I'm trying to be nice here, but you're not being very open to me right now."

I barked a sarcastic laugh. "You're right, how thoughtless of me. I'll take notes so next time you dump me, I'm more gracious about it."

He sighed. "Don't be like this."

I crossed my arms over my chest. "I'll be however the hell I want. You don't get to make demands anymore."

He shrugged. "Okay. Sure. I guess you're right."

Damn straight I was right. Ryan was *dumping* me. I suddenly realized there was no reason I had to be here. He'd said his piece—we were over. He'd already explained that he wasn't ready to make a commitment. There was nothing left for me to do or say here.

I stood to leave.

"Wait," Ryan said. "We're not going Dutch on the check?"

My mouth dropped. "Get the check yourself, asshole," I said and turned around, marching away from him.

I bit back my sobs until I was out of the bar where we'd met, and at least halfway down the road to the bus stop. When the tears finally rolled down my cheeks, a sob racked my throat.

I fished for my phone and called June.

"He dumped me," I sobbed into the phone.

"What? Izzy, oh, my God!"

"I know," I said. "He invited me out for drinks. We had a beer, and then we ate that greasy pub food I love so much. And *then* he dumped me. After we'd had a good afternoon together."

"I can't believe it," June said. "I have to get Bernie into this call, too."

I nodded, waiting for June to dial Bernadette into the call so we were on a three-way. My two best friends were saints, always there for me when shit hit the fan.

2

And shit had just hit the fan in a big way.

We were all in college together. I was in the art program, June studied communications and Bernie was going to be a teacher, but we'd shared a dorm room the first year and we'd been attached at the hip ever since.

"Izzy, are you okay?" Bernie asked when she hopped on the line. "June told me before connecting me."

"I'm fine," I lied. I felt like collapsing on the curb in a puddle of tears.

"He doesn't deserve you," Bernie said fiercely.

"I stuck him with the check this time. We usually split it," I said. For some reason, I felt bad about doing that. But that was my problem—I was too *nice*. I always ended up getting walked over because I was nice and I didn't want people to go out of their way for me. So, I ended up putting myself second.

All the time.

I was a secondary character in my own story when I should have been the main character who took all the glory.

And this just proved it. Not even Ryan wanted to be with me anymore.

"It's good you made him pay," June said. "I wish you could have stuck it to him more, really made his life hell somehow."

Bernie agreed.

"I don't want to make his life hell," I said. "I just... want to move on."

That wasn't going to be so easy. I was still in love with Ryan. Hell, until half an hour ago, I hadn't even known anything was wrong between us. I was just starting my last year at college, and he finished last year. We'd been talking about moving in together, about seeing what the rest of our lives would hold. I'd been ready for the long haul with him.

And he hadn't been able to see past today.

I swallowed down a sob.

3

"Do you know what you need?" June asked. "A rebound," she added before I could guess. "You need to get out there and get in bed with a hottie that will make you forget all about that idiot."

"Excellent idea! Don't waste any time on that loser," Bernie agreed enthusiastically.

"I don't know, you guys…" I wasn't really the type to sleep around. I was a long-term relationship gal through and through. One-night stands weren't my thing.

"We should go out," Bernie suggested. "We can drown your sorrows in alcohol. When you're too drunk to judge if the guy is hot enough to take home with you, we'll help you decide." She sounded triumphant.

"I'm working tonight," I said.

I reached the bus stop and glanced at the other people waiting to get on board. There were only two. One had earphones in his ears, and wouldn't hear my conversation. The other was reading a book.

"Come on," June groaned. "Cancel your shift."

"I can't do that. Besides, I'm saving up money for…" I didn't know how to finish that sentence. I'd been saving up money so that Ryan and I could get a place after college. Now, that wasn't going to happen. But *I* would still need a place to stay, whether it was with him or not. My stomach turned and I felt sick. God, all of this was so unexpected. And so *unfair*.

The bus rumbled toward us.

"I have to go," I said. "I'm working my shift, and then I'm going to bed. We'll talk tomorrow."

The girls protested about not being able to take me out for a short while longer, but then they gave in, and I ended the call. I climbed onto the bus, feeling numb, and I sat in one of the seats close to the back. I leaned my head against the window and watched the city slide by as the bus snaked through the streets of Los Angeles, taking me back to my student housing.

My shift at Café Noir started at five, and it ran until one in the morning. The café was a simple place during the day, offering food and artisan coffee. At night, we whipped out the cocktail menus and craft beers, and the crowd shifted from sensible daytime workers to raucous students.

I liked working there—it always had a good vibe, and since I'd worked at the café almost as long as I'd been studying, it felt like a home away from home.

"Hey, Izzy," my coworker Jimmy said when I clocked in for my shift and he clocked out. "Are you okay? You look…"

"I'm okay," I said before he could finish his sentence. "Just a tough week with classes and tests."

"You have some days off coming up soon, right? Then you can rest," he said.

"Yeah, that's a good point," I agreed, and he gave me a sympathetic smile before he left.

I walked to the counter, ready to serve the customers coming in for the late afternoon rush, and tried not to think about Ryan at all.

It would be no use if I cried into someone's coffee. That was just unprofessional.

Time ticked on and the orders changed from coffee to cocktails when the dinner orders started coming in. I worked hard, running back and forth, focusing on work so that I didn't have to think about anything else. My mind kept jumping to Ryan, and when I forced it away, I thought about what June and Bernie had suggested—a rebound. But I couldn't do that.

Could I?

I'd been in a two-year relationship until today. I'd been thinking long term. My mind had been on the future, not on the present, and not on getting my physical needs met. Instant gratification had been the last thing I'd wanted.

I felt like the rug had been ripped out from under me.

"Two black coffees, and the best stout you have on tap," a deep voice said. I looked up.

Oh. My. God.

The bluest eyes I'd ever seen pierced me, and they were set in a face that could only have been carved by the angels. He was the epitome of tall, dark, and handsome, with tanned skin that made him look like he went for morning runs on the beach, broad shoulders, a confident attitude, and a grin on his face that made my stomach flutter.

"Coming right up," I managed to say, which was a damn miracle because the sight of Mr. Hot-as-Hell had made me feel all tongue-tied. I turned away from him and started preparing his order. Two coffees and a stout—that was the order, right? Good thing he'd said it before I'd seen his face because I wouldn't have heard a word he said.

What was wrong with me? I didn't usually notice guys like this. But if they looked like *him,* I'm sure I would have looked twice. Relationship or not.

When I'd prepared the two coffees, I put them on the counter.

He smiled at me and my heart skipped a beat.

"Let me just get that beer," I said.

He nodded, and I walked to the beer taps to pour the stout. I took the pint glass to the counter and put it down, calculating the price in my mind.

He pulled out a handful of bills and smiled at me again.

Cue the butterflies.

"Keep the change," he said.

"Thanks. Here you go," I said, offering him a tray for the coffee and the beer so that he wouldn't have to juggle them all.

"Thanks," he said. He flashed me that grin and walked away.

The conversation had been simple. But I shivered, my stomach tightening again, and I watched him walk to a table with another man and a woman.

My stomach sank a little. Was he taken?

I snuck glances at him the rest of the night while I worked, watching the body language of his group. They were too far away from the counter for me to hear what they were saying, and as the evening picked up and I got busier, I could focus on them less and less. But at some point, the other man leaned over and kissed the woman, and I was oddly satisfied.

They were a couple. Mr. Dreamy was a third wheel.

Which didn't by any means tell me he was single—a man *that* attractive had to have a woman who was supermodel material. But still, a girl could hope.

They stood and left, and my stomach sank again when the table was empty. I would have liked to at least talk to him again.

But men like him didn't happen to women like me.

Just as well. I didn't need to get hurt another time.

It would have been nice, though, if at least one thing in my life worked out the way it did in the movies. Since I'd already lost my happy ending and all, I was due for some sort of good luck.

I wiped down the counter while I waited for the next person to order. It was getting close to midnight and business was dying down. We were closing up soon. And then I just had to help clean up before I could go home.

Someone walked up to the counter and cleared his throat.

When I looked up, I froze. Once again, I was caught in the gaze of Mr. Blue Eyes.

CHAPTER 2

CARTER

*F*uck, she was cute. Not just cute, smoldering hot, too. But something about the way she looked at me, the way her mouth perpetually looked like it wanted to curl into a smile, made me want to talk to her.

"Hi, Isabelle," I said when she looked up at me, blinking like I was some kind of vision.

She glanced down at her name tag, which was where I'd found out her gorgeous name. Then she looked back up at me.

"Hi," she said. "Can I... can I get you something? I think our kitchen is closed, but..." She looked over her shoulder at the kitchen. She was flustered, and that made her even more attractive.

And she was already a stunner, with red hair that hung over her shoulder in light curls, and big, round brown eyes that made me want to fall into them.

"Yeah," I said. "Your number."

She blinked at me. "What?"

"I'm a little forward," I said. "Sorry about that. You're just the most beautiful thing I've seen in a long, long time.

And I can't pass up the opportunity to spend some time with you."

She blinked at me before her cheeks flushed.

"I'm not a *thing*," she bristled.

I laughed. Oh, God. Feisty, too. She was the whole package.

"I just told you you're beautiful, and all you heard was that I said *thing?*"

She shrugged. "I don't like being treated like the help."

I laughed again. "I wasn't trying to treat you like the help. Poor choice of words. You're the most beautiful *woman* I've seen in a long, long time. Is that better?"

She bit her lip, then nodded shyly.

Shit. Already, she was driving me wild. I smiled.

"And I do want to spend some time with you. Would you like to have a drink with me?"

She hesitated.

"There's still time before you close, right?" I asked.

"I'm not allowed to drink on the job," she said.

"Who's going to know?" I asked. "We're the only ones left."

When she looked around, she saw I was right. There weren't any other patrons left. Everyone had gone home for the night. It was five minutes to twelve, and there was still time for her to pour another couple of beers.

She turned it over in her mind, I could see her thinking. And it was hot as hell.

"Okay," she finally said.

I grinned at her. "Okay."

She disappeared and a moment later, she returned with two beers.

We walked to the table where I'd sat with my college pal, Ray, and his girlfriend, Sonya.

"So, Isabelle," I said when we sat down.

"Most people call me Izzy," she said. "The name tag is formal." She touched her fingers to the tag on her chest.

"Izzy." Sassy. I liked it. "I'm Carter."

She smiled. "Hi, Carter."

I smiled at the sound of my name on her lips.

"So, Izzy, what do you do? Besides work here?"

"I'm a student," she said. "Art major."

I whistled through my teeth. "That's impressive."

"Is it?"

"For sure," I said. She looked shy under the compliment.

I had a lot of respect for art students. It was a difficult career path—it was all about passion to them because most of them didn't make it far in the art world. Making money from something like that, no matter how passionate you were about it, was hard.

"What about you?" she asked.

"I finished college last year. I'm just wrapping up an internship now."

"So, what's next for you, then?" she asked.

I took a swig of beer. "Business school."

"Really?"

I nodded. "I want to make a difference, you know? But not in the way most people say they want to."

"How, then?"

"Gourmet food."

She laughed, and I was in trouble. I could get addicted to that sound.

"Hey," I said, poking her lightly in the shoulder and loving the contact. "Good food brings people together. And it makes a profitable business, too."

"I like your enthusiasm. Where's your school?" she asked.

"New York."

Was it my imagination, or did her face fall?

I was flying out to New York City in two days to start

graduate school. I'd worked hard to get where I was now, and I'd work even harder when I got to the Big Apple.

"When are you leaving?" she asked.

I hesitated, unsure if I should tell her. I didn't want to scare her off.

"In two days."

Her eyes widened. "Oh, that's soon."

I nodded.

Leaving was bittersweet. I loved LA, but I needed to take this next step. An MBA would open a lot of doors for me. And I had big plans.

"Well, I'm sure you'll do well in grad school," Izzy said. "It sounds like you're passionate about your future business."

I nodded. "Absolutely. What's the point if there's no passion?"

"Exactly," she said. "That's why I'm studying art, even though I know what most people say about it."

"I think it's noble," I said. "What kind of art do you make?"

"I'm a painter," she said, her eyes lighting up.

"Ah. What do you like to paint?"

"Anything," she said, playing with a lock of her fire-red hair. "Landscapes, abstract. But portraits are my favorite. I love people's faces. They always tell a story."

She smiled at me. Her eyes were mesmerizing. I knew I was leaving soon, but I wanted to get to know her better. Something about her made me want to get closer, to find out what made her tick.

"Are you single?" I asked.

My question surprised me as much as it surprised her.

"Yeah," she said, and an expression flickered across her face too fast for me to read.

"Lucky me," I said and grinned at her.

She laughed, and it was beautiful. Rich and full and genuine.

"Yeah, I guess you are."

I took a sip of my beer. "So, what are you doing when you're not working at Café Noir or painting pictures?"

"Being a full-time student and working take up most of my time," she admitted.

"What are you doing tonight?" I asked.

She shrugged. "After locking up and erasing all signs of my breaking the rules right now—" she winked at me "—I'm probably going to go home and get a good night's sleep so that I'm up early for classes again tomorrow."

"That's too bad," I said.

"Why?"

"Because I was hoping you would come out with me to celebrate."

She blinked at me. "What are we celebrating?"

"The fact that I met the most beautiful woman I've ever seen." I grinned at her and watched as she blushed bright red.

"Oh, you are smooth, Carter. But meeting me is hardly cause for celebration."

"Oh, Isabelle," I said, leaning forward. "Have you *seen* you?"

She blushed again and I reached forward, touching her arm. I couldn't help myself. She was magnetic.

"So, what do you say?" I asked. "When you're done here, do you want to come with me?"

"Where are we going?" she asked in a breathy voice.

"Wherever you want."

"For someone who looks so put together, I'd think you'd have an answer ready for that question," she said.

I laughed. "You think I look put together?"

"Don't you?" she asked. "I mean, look at you." She slid her eyes over my body, and I relished the way she looked at me. "You're definitely the type of guy to command a boardroom."

I laughed. "Is it that obvious that I'm a business major? I couldn't pass for a carpenter, or a lumberjack?"

She raised her eyebrows. "Seriously? A lumberjack? I can just picture you in flannels and boots, sizing up a tree, wondering how much you'll have to bribe it to fall over for you."

I burst out laughing. "Bribe it?"

"Well, I can tell you work out," she said, blushing. "But you don't have the callused hands of someone who runs a chainsaw for a living." She reached for me and took my hand in both of hers. At the contact, electricity jumped between us and my breath caught in my throat. She glanced up at me before studying my hand.

I loved the feel of her hands on mine, her skin soft and smooth, and her fingers able. She had paint spots on her hands, and the splotches were endearing.

I leaned forward so that our heads were bowed together, studying my hand.

"So, you think I'll be better at closing deals than chopping down trees?" I asked. My voice was a little hoarse.

She glanced up at me again and her face was so close to mine, I could see the flecks of gold dancing in those big brown eyes.

"Yeah. And it's better for the environment."

I chuckled. I could smell her shampoo. I lifted my free hand and tucked her hair behind her ear. Her eyes were locked on mine, and when I leaned in to kiss her, she closed her eyes.

When our lips touched, it was the same incredible electrical surge that pulsed through me as when she'd touched my hand. I slid my tongue into her mouth and she moaned softly.

The sound was erotic, and it made my cock stiffen in my pants.

I cupped her cheek and kissed her more urgently, trying to show her the effect she was having on me. I moved my hands to her back, sliding them over her shoulders and up to her hair as I pulled her closer. Her arms wrapped around my shoulders. I inhaled her scent, intoxicated.

When we finally broke apart to look at each other, she was out of breath as if she'd run a mile, and her eyes were darker, deeper. Her lips were slightly parted.

"Come home with me," I said.

She leaned back a little.

Shit, did I blow it?

"I have to clean up and lock up the café," she said.

I nodded. "I'll help you."

We stood together. All the other employees had gone home, and I helped her close up. We tipped the chairs onto the tables for the cleaning crew to come in the morning, wiped the counters down, and she switched on the large industrial dishwasher that someone had loaded earlier.

The whole time, I couldn't stop staring at her. I watched her as she moved, keeping track of her as we worked. She was elegant and graceful, doing everything with care, as if it really mattered. Her long red hair was like a flame as she moved beneath the dim lights. When she glanced at me now and again, her eyes were deep. Her expression suggested she was as eager about getting out of here as I was.

When the shop was ready, and she'd locked the door, she turned to me.

"I don't usually do this," she announced.

"What? Have help cleaning up the shop?"

She giggled. "No. Go home with someone I just met. It's not usually… my style."

"Okay," I said. What if she changed her mind? I desperately needed her, but I didn't want to persuade her to do something she didn't want. "Are you sure you want to do this?"

"Yes, I am. But I just wanted you to know that."

I nodded. "Noted. And I'm honored."

She nodded, too.

"So, which way?" she asked.

I took her hand and lifted it to my mouth, brushing my lips against her knuckles.

"This way," I breathed and led her to my car.

CHAPTER 3

ISABELLE

I was going home with him.

I hardly recognized myself. A one-night stand? And what was more, I was fresh out of a long-term relationship. That was who I was— *the* long-term relationship girl.

And where had that gotten me?

Dumped, and feeling like crap because for some reason, Ryan just didn't think I was good enough to commit to.

And that was totally bullshit.

Maybe I wasn't like some of the other girls who ran around campus, who had a ton of friends and big trust funds, but I had some good things going for me.

And Carter could see that. He talked to me like I was worth something.

I realized that for a long time, Ryan had made me feel like I wasn't worth much at all. I had just been so caught up in our dream of 'forever' that I hadn't noticed how he'd started disregarding me, and how he'd started treating me like I was a *maybe* in his life, when he'd been a *definitely* in mine all that time.

Carter looked at me like I was the only woman in the

world. Even though it was just for tonight, the way he treated me felt *good*.

We rode with the windows down. He moved his hand to my leg and interlinked his fingers with mine. It was sexy, but sweet, too. Everything about him, every little move he made, was perfect.

His car was nice. Expensive, but not in a flashy way. I liked that about him—he was obviously higher on the economic food chain, and he had a few doors already open for him in life. But he didn't give me the idea that it defined him. He didn't rub it in my face or make me think he was just using it to get me in bed.

And that made me want to get in bed with him all the more.

Still, Carter was a stranger. And I didn't go home with strangers. I'd always had a theory that going home with strangers was asking for trouble. But when I thought about Ryan, I realized that even though I'd thought I knew him all this time, it turned out that I really hadn't known him all that well. I would have never thought he would throw away something we'd worked on for so long...

For no reason at all.

And Carter... there was something about him that made him feel like he wasn't a stranger at all. When we talked, it was like he *understood* me. And I hadn't had that with anyone.

Not with Ryan, and not with any of the guys I'd dated before.

Not even with my girlfriends, to be honest. Not like this. I'd always figured it was because I was an artist. A little different from everyone else. I hadn't expected anyone to truly understand me.

But somehow, it felt like Carter did.

And that wasn't something I wanted to let slip through my fingers.

So when he'd asked me if I wanted to go home with him, the only answer that had made logical sense was 'yes.'

We arrived at his apartment and he unlocked the door, letting me walk in first.

"Oh," I said when he flicked on the lights and I looked around. "This place doesn't look anything like my student apartment."

My place was a little dingy, with water damage on the ceiling, an oven I had to wedge shut with a broomstick, and a door I had to put my body weight behind to open or shut if I wanted to come or go.

Carter's place was neatly outfitted with modern designer furniture, and it had a clean, masculine scent.

Carter chuckled when I ogled the place.

"It's not much, but it's home."

"Are you kidding me?" I asked. "If this is your definition of 'not much,' I don't want to know what the rest of your life will look like when you're some crazy business mogul."

I shrugged out of my coat and Carter took it for me. A real gentleman.

He laughed. "You think I'm going to become a business mogul?"

"Oh, yes," I said.

He certainly looked the part. I was pretty sure he would be drop-dead gorgeous in a designer suit.

He was already jump-his-bones hot.

All he needed was to take that commanding air a step further and he was going to be *everything*.

He cupped my cheek, his face close to mine.

"You're staring," he mumbled, his lips so close to mine I could barely concentrate on the words he was speaking.

"You're distracting," I said.

I sounded like a fool. But he chuckled, and his voice was thick and smooth and it caressed my skin like honey.

When he kissed me, it was just as electric as it had been at the café when he'd pressed his lips against mine. But this time, it was different. There was so much more passion behind it. So much more *lust*. He pressed the length of his body against mine, and I could feel the bulge in his pants, proof of his growing interest in me.

And God, I wanted him. He was charming and handsome and confident—exactly the type of guy I never expected to end up with. And what was more, he wanted me, too.

I could feel it all the way down in his boxers, where his cock strained against his pants to get to me.

It was setting my body on fire, the way he ground himself against me. My stomach tightened. I was getting wet for him.

God, *so* wet.

Carter broke the kiss and looked at me.

"Can I get you something to drink?" he asked.

Was he serious? I didn't want anything to drink. Or to eat. Or *anything* that wasn't him naked and on top of me.

I blushed at myself, thinking things like this about a total stranger.

But then again, he didn't feel like a stranger to me.

I shook my head and kissed him, running my hands over his chest.

"I want to know where your bedroom is," I said.

He chuckled against my mouth and wrapped his arms around me. His hands landed on my ass and he picked me up. I yelped. He lifted me as if I weighed no more than a feather, and when I held onto his shoulders, I could feel the muscles ripple as he held me up. I wrapped my legs around his waist and he carried me to the bedroom. His tongue was in my mouth again and I moaned softly, only vaguely aware of the apartment around us as he moved me to the bedroom.

He didn't bother with the lights—the bedroom was illuminated enough with light pouring in from the other rooms

—and he placed me on the bed. I giggled for some reason then. I felt delirious with desire. He smiled at me.

He was on top of me in a flash, kissing me, his hands roaming my body, touching me, tracing my curves with his fingers.

He pulled up my shirt, exposing my bra, and moved his head to my chest. He kissed a line along my bra cup, leaving a trail of fire on the tender skin of my breasts.

I tugged my shirt over my head, and arched my back when Carter tried to reach around me. He unclasped my bra and pulled it off, and I lay in front of him, topless.

For a moment, I was shy. No matter how immediately close I felt to him, he was still unknown to me. And I was suddenly as good as naked. His eyes slid over my breasts and then back to my face.

"You're gorgeous," he said.

I blushed and he leaned down to kiss me. He cupped my left breast, his fingers strong and sure, knowing exactly what he wanted. I moaned as he kneaded my breast, his fingers finding my erect nipple, and he rolled it between his thumb and forefinger.

I gasped and moaned, his attention to my breast sending electric jolts to my pussy, making me even wetter.

Carter dipped his head, breaking the kiss, and his mouth found my right nipple. He sucked it into his mouth and I moaned as he licked and sucked me, balancing me between his hand on one breast and his mouth on the other.

For a while, all I could do was lose myself in the sensation of Carter worshiping my body. He made me feel incredible. And we hadn't done anything below the belt yet—he was still fully dressed and I was still wearing my pants.

As if Carter knew that I'd been thinking it, he started moving down my body, kissing his way over my stomach. His fingers made quick work of unbuttoning my jeans, and he slowly peeled them down my legs, as if he was unwrapping a gift. Slowly. Sensually, *deliciously*.

His fingers were hot on my skin when he got rid of my jeans and ran his hands up my legs. He parted my thighs, and breathed hot air on me.

I moaned and curled on the bed.

When he closed his mouth over me and flicked his tongue over my clit, I cried out.

I pushed my hands into his hair, grabbing fistfuls and curling my fingers through his thick, dark hair.

Carter started lapping at the delicate folds of my sex, licking and sucking and pushing me closer and closer to the edge of an orgasm.

I trembled and squirmed on the bed, pulling his head against my pussy, bucking my hips as I got closer and closer.

When he pushed two fingers into me, it was what I needed to topple over the edge. Pleasure washed over me. I cried out and closed my legs around Carter's head. He chuckled, and his deep voice reverberated through my body, settling at my core as I came.

When I came down from my sexual bliss, Carter pushed up onto his knees and pulled his shirt over his head. I ogled his body.

God, he was *hot*. Chiseled as fuck, every individual muscle carved and beautiful. He was an Adonis, carved by the angels and sent to Earth for women like me to drool over.

He chuckled when I couldn't stop staring.

"You're like a *GQ* magazine model," I said, and felt like an idiot for saying it. I blushed, but Carter only laughed.

I sat up and started working on his pants. I undid the button on his jeans, pulled the zipper down, and set his cock free.

And *God*, he was delicious. Impressive, straining, silk over steel, and his tip was slick with his lust for me.

I glanced up at him.

He kissed me again, leaning down, cupping my cheeks, and gently nudged me back so that I lay on my back. He crawled over me, and my legs fell open for him.

When his cock pressed against my entrance, I held my breath, and let it out in a long moan when he pushed into me.

Fuck, he felt *incredible.*

I trembled, my muscles clenching tightly around the size of him.

Carter started moving, and I forgot about everything around us. All that existed in this moment was me and Carter and the absolute pleasure that exploded in my center when he started moving in and out of me.

I gripped his shoulders when he started fucking me. He was in total control, pumping his hips, sliding his cock in and out of me, and I was along for the ride. My fingers dug into his skin and I cried out with every thrust as he sank deeper and deeper into me.

The sensation started building another orgasm inside me. I gave myself over to the pleasure as I came undone at the seams.

When I orgasmed again, my body clamped down on his cock and Carter grunted, slowing his pace until he stroked in and out of me torturously slowly.

When I recovered from my second orgasm, breathing hard, he leaned down and kissed me.

"Get on top of me," he said.

"What?"

He kissed me another time, so deeply I couldn't think straight.

"I want you to ride me."

I shivered at the way he said it. His voice was commanding, his eyes a piercing blue, and I wanted to give him exactly what he wanted. Just as I wanted to take what I needed.

I'd never had sex like this, so intense, so connected and sensual.

Carter rolled onto his back, his cock standing up in the air, ready for me to mount him. I clambered onto him and when I lowered myself onto his cock, we groaned in unison.

"You're so fucking tight," he said through gritted teeth.

"It's you," I replied, gasping, "your size is… incredible."

He chuckled, but it was cut short when he pulled me down and kissed me. While our lips were locked and our tongues swirled around each other, I started moving back and forth, sliding his cock in and out of me.

I rocked harder, faster, moaned when he penetrated me, deeper and deeper.

I moaned and cried out as I rocked faster and harder, closing my eyes, *feeling* him.

When I opened my eyes, his were locked on mine. He clenched his jaw, and a look of intense concentration crossed his face.

He grabbed my hips and helped me, rocking me back and forth harder and further than I was able to go myself. It was magic. My clit rubbed against his pubic bone and I was well on the way to my third orgasm.

Carter gritted his teeth, moaning and groaning, and I could see the need in his face, the urgency.

He was getting close.

I wanted him to come. I wanted to push him over the edge so that he released and found the same pleasure he'd given me.

For a moment, I was focused on him, but the friction on my clit pushed me over the edge. I cried out as I orgasmed yet again.

I closed my eyes and opened my mouth in a raw cry of pleasure.

Carter cried out a moment later, and I felt him releasing inside me, pumping and throbbing, his cock dumping all the pleasure we'd built into my body.

I collapsed on his chest, and Carter wrapped himself around me, holding onto me for dear life as he pumped into me.

We stayed like this for a while after the climax subsided, clinging together. Our skin was slick with sweat and we were so close, I wasn't sure where I ended and he began.

I'd never had anything like this. Nothing that made me feel like it was me, like it was about more than sex. And I'd never had anything that made me feel so incredible.

When I lifted my head, Carter smiled sleepily at me. "That was so good."

"It was," I agreed.

I rolled off him and lay next to him, feeling sleep overcome me, too.

"The bathroom is right there," Carter said, pointing.

I nodded and rolled off the bed, walking to the bathroom to clean up. Carter had left a sticky mess between my legs.

After cleaning up, I walked back to the bed. Carter was in it, and he flipped the covers back so I could get in with him.

"You want me to stay?" I asked.

"Absolutely," he said, and I climbed into bed.

Everything was so perfect. It was almost too good to be true. How did it work that the same day I'd lost what I thought was my entire future, I found someone like Carter?

It had to mean something.

Coming home with him was the best decision I'd ever made.

Carter reached for me, wrapped his arm around my body

and pulled me close to him. He curled his body around me protectively and sighed.

I closed my eyes, relishing his warmth.

For now, this was good.

I wasn't sure what would happen with the new light of day, but for now, it was exactly what I needed.

CHAPTER 4

CARTER

I opened my eyes and blinked against the bright light that fell through open curtains. Usually, they were closed and I could sleep in, but today I was up bright and early.

And my bed was empty.

I frowned and lifted my head, looking at the spot where the covers were turned back. The spot where Izzy had fallen asleep last night.

Where the hell was she? And why wasn't she still in my bed, cuddling up to me?

I sat up and rubbed my eyes, trying to listen for a sound from the rest of the apartment. When I got up and walked through the rooms, I realized her clothes and her purse were gone.

She's left.

Fuck.

I walked back to the bedroom and found my phone. She hadn't given me her number. I checked anyway, making sure she hadn't left it for me while I was sleeping.

What time had she gotten up to leave? It was only seven now.

I sat on the bed and ran my hands through my hair, irritated that she was gone and I had no way of contacting her.

This wasn't new. I fucked girls often, and sent them packing the next day. But this time, I hadn't asked her to leave. She'd been the one to do that.

And the worst part was that I hadn't exactly wanted her to leave.

The realization traveled through me with a shock.

Since when did I want women to stick around? I was serious about school, and I was leaving tomorrow to go to New York. I wasn't looking to get involved with anyone. Besides, relationships were nothing but trouble. It was easier to fuck them and let them go again without any strings attached.

But with Izzy, everything had been different. I'd felt a connection with her unlike anything I'd felt before.

And not just in bed, either. I'd felt connected to her while we were talking in the café. Hell, I'd felt that spark between us the moment I placed my order with her. I'd just had to talk to her again.

And when I had, it turned out that she was amazing in every way possible.

Apparently in bed, too.

And now, she was gone.

My phone rang. Austin's name popped up on the caller ID.

"Are you awake?" he asked.

"I am."

"Breakfast?"

"Sure."

"I'll meet you at Farina."

"Let's do Café Noir," I said.

27

Austin agreed, and I showered and got dressed to meet him.

An hour later, Austin and I sat at the table where Izzy and I had talked last night. I glanced toward the counter where everyone placed their orders, but it didn't look like she was working.

But she'd worked late last night, so her absence made sense. Still, I was disappointed. I felt a growing sense of uneasiness.

Austin and I had grown up together, and I was getting into business with him, too. He was going to NYC with me so that we could start this thing together.

He was the one person I could talk to about anything.

"So, ready to get rolling?" he asked after we ordered coffee and a breakfast special with scrambled eggs, sausage, bacon, the works.

"Yeah…"

"That doesn't sound very convincing," Austin said.

The waitress brought us our coffees.

"Excuse me," I said to her. "I met a woman here last night, a waitress. Isabelle. Izzy. Is there any way I can get in touch with her?"

The waitress frowned at me. "Would you like to lodge a complaint? Or a compliment? You can talk to our manager."

"No," I said, shaking my head. "I just want to talk to her. Personally. I didn't get her contact details when I saw her and I'd like to get in touch."

"We're not allowed to hand out personal information," she said tightly.

"Come on, Gloria," I said, reading her name tag. "Give a guy a break."

Her frown grew tighter.

"I don't think so. Now can I get you anything else to eat?"

I shook my head sadly, and she disappeared.

Austin looked at me over the rim of his coffee cup.

"What was that all about?" he asked after setting the cup down.

I shrugged. "It's just a girl I met here... I was hoping I could see her again. Or stay in touch."

"Like... in a relationship?"

I shook my head. "No. I mean, I'm going to the other side of the country. That wouldn't make sense. I just..."

I wasn't sure what I wanted her number for, but it felt wrong to let something so incredible slip through my fingers. Nothing with her had been normal. It had felt so good. So right. Being with her had felt like being home.

And I wanted that back. I wanted to be able to hold onto that.

"So, it was a one-night stand?" Austin asked.

I nodded. "I guess that's all it was."

"You're better off not having contact, man," Austin said. "You don't need any strings attached right now, not as you're about to jet off to a new city thousands of miles away. It's better this way."

I nodded. Maybe Austin was right. It was better to not see her again.

And yet, I couldn't stop thinking about her.

After breakfast, I went back home to pack a few things and make a few calls to finalize the last things before I left. The movers came at noon, and they took all my furniture in one big truck, destined for a storage unit. I followed them in my car and helped unload everything into the climate-controlled unit. I remembered what Izzy had said to me.

You don't have the hands of someone who runs a chainsaw for a living.

I chuckled. She'd been so quick-witted, and I loved that about her.

If only you could see me now, Isabelle, I thought. *Moving heavy furniture and doing manual labor with the best of them.*

Had she thought of me as a spoiled rich kid? Lots of people thought that. As if I didn't have a clue about the real world because of my wealth.

The *real* world.

Sure, I was rich, but I knew a thing or two about life. It was easy to hate a rich guy, but they didn't know the whole story. Not half of it.

When I finished up and drove home, it was last afternoon, and I still couldn't stop thinking about Isabelle.

It wasn't just that the sex with her had been amazing. Everything about her was amazing. And I hadn't had that in a long time—if ever. I wanted to talk to her at least another time.

I wanted to get her number so that we could stay in touch. I was going to study in New York, but LA was my home. I'd still come back for visits.

When everything was taken care of at the apartment, I drove back to Café Noir. Her shift had been late afternoon yesterday. I was hoping I would run into her again, so that I could get her number. So that we could talk.

So she could tell me why she'd left so early without even saying goodbye.

Hell, something like that would have made me happy if it was any other woman. Having to tell them to leave was always such a pain in the ass, and most of the time, they wanted more when I wasn't willing to give it.

Now, I'd met the one woman I would have liked to see again, and she was the one that managed to slip away.

It hit me like a fucking ton of bricks.

I walked into the café and sat down at a table on the other side of the floor. I ordered a late lunch and a beer, and watched the people who came and went. After a while, a new shift of servers came to replace the old ones.

Still no Isabelle.

I stayed until well after the dinner rush, and finally realized that I was being an idiot.

She wasn't going to come in tonight.

And I had to get back home so that I could be ready to catch my flight first thing in the morning. My apartment had come partially furnished, so I had a bed to sleep on and a TV to break up the silence.

Putting her out of my mind was a disappointment. I'd really hoped I was going to see her again, even if it was just for a conversation, a coffee or something, to cap off the time we'd spent together.

With her leaving without a goodbye, it was so open-ended. And I would have liked to spend more time with her.

I would have liked to take a long shower the next morning, running my hands over her soapy body before getting breakfast together, instead of finding my bed empty. I would have liked to get to know more about who she was, and where she was headed in life.

The one night I'd had with Izzy just hadn't been enough.

But there was nothing I could do about it now.

I climbed into my car and drove back to my apartment. I grabbed a beer out of my fridge and wandered around the place, making sure everything was packed and ready. I'd already said goodbye to all my friends in LA at the going-away party for Austin and me two days earlier. I'd kept my last day in town free to take care of any last-minute details that arose.

Now here I was, on my last night in LA, and I was all alone.

After flicking through the TV channels and finding nothing to watch, I ended up going to bed.

My mind was filled with her, but I pushed the thoughts away.

Tomorrow, I was going to New York, and then I probably wouldn't see Izzy ever again.

Better to treat it like all the other hookups I'd had—forget about it.

I'd gotten what I wanted, which was to sleep with her. And that was it. She'd gotten the same.

The fact that there had been so much more between us than just sex?

Well, I'd have to stop thinking about that.

Sometimes, these little amazing things came across our paths, but they weren't meant to be.

Maybe it was the same with Izzy.

It had to be.

I couldn't bear the other possibility—that I'd just lost someone amazing.

CHAPTER 5

A couple of weeks passed, and I couldn't put Carter out of my mind.

But I had so much other shit to deal with, too, like the breakup with Ryan.

Besides, Carter had left. There was no reason for me to keep thinking about him.

He and I had had a magical night together, but it had been a one-night stand. No matter how incredible it had been, and what it had shown me I'd missed during my relationship with Ryan, it hadn't erased the fact that my life had somehow fallen apart in the blink of an eye.

And despite all that, Carter was all I could think about.

"You should call him," June said. We sat at Farina, a café on the other end of the neighborhood from where I worked. When I had days off, the last place I wanted to be was Café Noir.

"I can't," I said, popping a potato fry into my mouth. "I don't have his number."

"I can't believe you haven't made an effort to find him yet," June said. "After what you told me about him, he's

33

amazing in every way. And that's totally what you need. Not that loser Ryan."

"I know," I said. "But I still have to deal with the breakup. I mean, I need to get over Ryan, you know? I can't just jump headfirst into another relationship if I haven't really gotten over the first one. I wouldn't want someone like Carter to be a rebound. He's too *perfect* to screw it up like that." I swished another fry through a puddle of ketchup. "Besides, he left. Remember? No point in pursuing something that *can't* happen."

June took a sip of her soda and nodded. "Yeah, okay. I get that. You're totally noble. It's just weird that he's so great, and you don't want to contact him."

I shrugged.

The truth was, I *had* looked for him. The two days after my night with him, I went to the café outside my working hours, hoping I would bump into him.

But I had studies to focus on, a future to build with the money I was saving up. It was as if Carter had never existed in reality. He was just a magical memory from a night carved out somewhere in the sands of time.

Finding him on social media was impossible. I didn't even have a last name to go by.

"Tell me again why you left that morning before he woke up?" June asked.

I rolled my eyes. She was still adamant that I should have at least woken him up instead of just disappearing like that. But I'd woken up next to him and felt terrible for sleeping with him. Not because it had been wrong, but because I'd been an emotional mess. It shouldn't have happened. Not like that, not just after a breakup.

That didn't mean it hadn't been the most amazing night of sex and connection, though.

That wasn't the point.

Plus, there was the fact that he'd been perfect. And that had scared me. Men like that didn't exist—they only *seemed* perfect until you got to know them.

And even though I'd looked for him, it was probably better this way. It was better that I moved on and did my own thing, and he did his own thing, and we kept it preserved in our memory as that one perfect night.

Or at least it had been one perfect night to me. I had no idea how he thought of it.

And it shouldn't have mattered since he was leaving.

Looking back, I did wish I'd stayed a little longer to spend more time with him. But it was in the past now—I'd made my decision. I'd left his bed in the early hours of the morning with the same clothes I'd worn the night before, and I'd hailed a cab on the street a block from his apartment.

"Well," June said after I explained to her exactly what I'd been thinking at the time, "the good thing is that it looks like you're moving on from Ryan. That asshole doesn't deserve a single tear cried over him."

"Yeah," I said, nodding. "I agree."

"Good."

"There is one thing I'm worried about," I admitted.

June looked up at me.

"My period is late."

She stilled. "Oh, my God. Are you serious? How late?"

"A while... I was waiting for it because sometimes it's a few days late. But, well, it's starting to become serious." I fidgeted with the napkin in my lap. I'd been trying not to think about this new development, but it was eating away at me.

June hesitated before her next question. "Do you know whose it is? I mean, if you're...you know, pregnant?"

I nodded. "It would be Carter's."

"But you broke up with Ryan that same day...don't you think...?"

I shook my head. "Things weren't so great between us. Ryan hadn't touched me the last month or two we were together. Honestly, I think he may have been cheating on me."

June looked shocked when she leaned forward. "Okay, first of all, Ryan is such an ass. And second of all...oh, my God, Izzy! You could be pregnant from a guy you hardly know!"

"It might just be a scare," I said.

I was hoping to God that was all it was because the alternative wasn't something I was ready to face.

"You have to get a test," June said.

I shook my head. "Absolutely not."

"Why not?" she asked. "You'll know for sure if you do. It's stupid, putting it off and stressing about whether or not your period is going to come."

I sighed. June was right, of course. She usually was.

"Okay," I agreed.

June's phone rang.

"It's Bernie," she announced, and she answered the call. I listened to June's side of the conversation, then gasped in surprise and shame when she told Bernie we were all going to the store to get a pregnancy test.

"You didn't have to do that," I said.

"Of course I did! Bernie wants to be there for you just like I do."

I shook my head. "It's so embarrassing."

"It's not," June said. "This shit happens. You have sex, sometimes you get pregnant. There's nothing wrong with that."

"Thank you," I said. My friends really were the greatest.

"I mean, condoms fail sometimes," she said as she pushed her plate away and glanced up at me.

I cringed.

"What? Izzy, you didn't use a condom?" she asked, horrified.

I cringed harder. "I know, I know. We were stupid. But I thought I was on an infertile day, and you know, I didn't want to ruin the moment."

"Izzy!" she gasped.

"I'm an idiot. What can I say?" I said, burying my face in my hands.

"You're not an idiot," she said, taking my hand. "It was a mistake. But let's find out how big that mistake was."

My stomach twisted in a knot of nerves as we got the check and left. What if I really was pregnant? What if this was real? I didn't know where to find Carter. But no, I scolded myself. One step at a time. Maybe it really was just a scare, and there was no reason to be worried.

We met Bernie outside the neighborhood grocery store, and after exchanging hugs, we walked to the aisle that stocked pregnancy tests. The tests were sandwiched between the condoms and the baby products.

"This has got to be some kind of joke," I said grimly, looking at the display. "A reminder on one side, the consequence on the other."

Bernie shook her head and looped her arm through mine. "They had to lump it together, no one wants to look for the condoms in the veggie aisle. It would make everyone uncomfortable seeing them right next to the cucumbers."

I burst out laughing. I was suddenly relieved my friends were both here to help me through this, and I didn't have to do it alone.

I bought a home pregnancy test, and we all marched to my apartment together.

We weren't roommates anymore—in our last year of studies, we were all in apartments of our own. But I was so glad the first-year dorms had thrown the three of us together. They were the best friends a woman could have.

"I'll be back," I said when I walked to the bathroom, leaving Bernie and June on my bed where they looked just as nervous as I felt.

I peed on the stick, replacing the cap after and walking back to the bedroom.

"Three minutes," I said. "And then the rest of my life might totally change."

"It's going to be okay," Bernie said, squeezing my hand.

"Yeah," June said. "No matter what, we're here for you. You're going to get through this."

"How do you know?" I asked with a shudder. The idea of having a baby was terrifying.

"Because you're like a cat, Izzy," Bernie said. "You always land on your feet. If the breakup with Ryan didn't prove it, the way you're working and studying like a madwoman sure does."

I nodded. My friends were right, I was going to get through this. And they were going to be here for me. I was so lucky to have them.

I just hoped that I wasn't pregnant. I could do anything I set my mind to, but that didn't mean I was ready to be a mom.

"It's time," June said when the timer on my phone beeped, and I took a deep breath. I walked to the bathroom where I'd left the test, and squeezed my eyes shut for a moment before I looked at the testing screen.

My heart dropped and I felt sick to my stomach.

"And?" June asked from the bedroom.

With trembling hands, I threw the test in the trash, hardly

knowing what I was doing. I walked into the room, feeling like I was going to faint.

They could see it all over my face. I didn't have to tell them.

"Oh, honey," Bernie said.

When I collapsed on the bed, they moved to either side of me and took my hands. Tears started rolling down my cheeks.

"I can't do this," I said. "I can't have a baby. Not now. I'm not ready."

"You have some time to prepare," June said. "And we're here. We'll figure this out, okay?"

I nodded, still crying. How was I going to raise a child? I still had another year of school left. What was I going to do? I couldn't raise a child as a student artist.

And what about the father? Where in the world was Carter now? He wasn't going to be able to help me with this. I had no idea where to find him.

"This is going to be so hard," I cried.

"I know," June said.

"But we're here," Bernie added. "And you can do it. You have it in your blood. You're not the first person to raise a baby alone."

They were right about that. My mom had raised me on her own. I wasn't sure if it was the same situation—she never wanted to talk about my dad. But she'd done it, and my life had been pretty good. She'd struggled, but she'd given me everything I truly needed.

And she'd done it alone.

Would she be disappointed that I was going to walk this road? I hoped not. I hoped that she would understand.

I'd never meant for any of this to happen. All I'd wanted was to spend a night with someone that would help me forget about my stupid ex-boyfriend, that would help me feel worth it. What had I done to deserve this?

Sure, it was stupid to not insist he use a condom. But this seemed like such a high price to pay for that mistake.

And now, this was what I got for it.

"Don't do that," June said.

"Do what?" I asked, wiping my cheeks with my sleeves.

"Don't blame yourself and think about how shitty your luck is."

My friends knew me too well.

"It's going to take some getting used to," Bernie said. "But you're going to be just fine."

"Because I'm a cat," I said, nodding. "I always land on my feet."

"Right," my friends agreed in unison.

I took a deep breath and let it out in a shudder.

It wasn't that simple. I knew they would be there for me. I knew that I could figure this out, somehow. But I felt awful that I was going to have a baby that would grow up without a father.

Still, I was going to figure this out. I would have to. I had no other choice—I wasn't going to be able to track Carter down.

"I'm going to have a baby," I said.

Saying the words out loud didn't make me feel like it was a sudden reality. It still felt crazy, surreal, impossible.

But I'd slept with Carter that night and we hadn't used protection. We should have, but we hadn't, and that was it.

Here I was.

I wasn't sure how I was going to do this, but I was going to do it the way I did everything else I wasn't sure about.

One day at a time, and eventually, I would figure it out.

I didn't have any other options.

CHAPTER 6

Five Years Later

*B*eing back in LA was a great change of scenery. After getting my master's degree in business, I'd been running Appetite, the gourmet food company I'd started in honor of my late mother who'd always dreamed of doing something like this.

Now, with a lot of money in my accounts and a company that was growing by the day, I was back in California to oversee some things at the LA branch. I had loose plans to stay in town for a few weeks. The New York offices could manage without me for a while.

Austin was with me, and he looked pleased as fucking punch.

"I don't know how you do this, man," he said. "You have the Midas Touch when it comes to business. I can't tell you how great it is to work together."

We waited in the boardroom at the Appetite headquarters for a meeting to commence.

"You're just inflating my ego," I said with a laugh.

"And rightfully so! With this deal, Appetite is going to skyrocket to the next level. And we were already in a different league."

I nodded. We were. The company had taken off better than expected when we started out, and we'd been seeing growth of more than two-hundred percent every year since we'd opened our doors.

Now, we were cementing a relationship with a group of investors who were willing to back our dreams of expanding across the country, turning Appetite into a franchise opportunity. Soon, there would be a branch in every major city, and once we pulled that off, we would be playing in the big leagues.

When the investors arrived, it was time to put on our business faces, and Austin and I got right into it. We discussed numbers, we were clear on what we were willing to bend on, and what not, and it didn't take all of two hours to wrap up business and get a bunch of contracts signed.

By the time the meeting ended, Appetite was in an even better position than where it started.

When we walked out, Austin clapped me on the back.

"You, my friend, are the next Bill Gates, Jeff Bezos, or Elon Musk."

I laughed and shook my head. "Don't compare me to giants. I'm just a humble millionaire, looking for a way to keep a dream alive."

Austin burst out laughing. "A *humble* millionaire! A fucking comedian is more like it." He laughed all the way out of the building, shaking his head. "What are we doing tonight?"

"Tonight?" I asked.

"Yeah, man. Don't tell me you're not going to celebrate this the way it deserves to be celebrated."

The truth was, I'd planned to go back to my hotel room

and sleep as much as I could. The past couple of months had been ridiculously busy, with me pulling late nights almost all week to get this ready so that we could catapult the business into the future.

I had to put effort in to get anything worth my while out, and I'd just about broken myself for this company.

I wanted to sleep and watch TV, before finally heading back to New York.

"I guess we could do something," I said.

"We're going to throw one hell of a party," Austin said. "We should book the Glasshouse, invite everyone we know, and do this right."

I groaned inwardly. It wasn't what I was in the mood for. But Austin wasn't wrong—a business deal this big *did* deserve to be celebrated.

"Okay," I said. "The Glasshouse it is. I'll get Beth to organize the whole thing, you just send invites to whoever you think should be there."

Austin nodded. "Sure. You do the same."

We agreed and parted ways. Austin had another business meeting to go to—he handled a lot of the PR side of my business, while I was more focused on the food and the finances. It worked well between us.

I called Beth and gave the instruction to book the Glasshouse, arrange caterers, the whole shebang. I knew it wasn't going to be easy on such short notice, but if there was anyone who could pull strings, it was my PA, and the Glasshouse was a restaurant we'd done business with before. Beth only had to mention my name and the upscale place would take care of it.

I climbed into the car that would take me back to my hotel, then I started scrolling through my contacts list. I was going to have to find someone to invite to the party. I had a few friends I still stayed in touch with on the West Coast and

I texted them, letting them know that something was going down tonight.

And then I started scrolling through the contacts of all the women I'd been with. I had most of their numbers, although I only vaguely remembered them. There had been so many of them, their faces and the nights we'd spent together started blurring into one mass of sex and women and alcohol.

Some people told me I was a womanizer for fucking around so much, for having one-night stands and never calling any of them again.

Maybe that was true. Maybe that did make me an asshole. But I never led them on, I never let them believe they were going to get anything else from me. Certainly never a commitment.

And when it was over, I was very clear with them that my mind hadn't changed.

If they couldn't deal with that, then it wasn't my problem. I wasn't the relationship type and I wasn't about to change who I was.

I just didn't build connections with people. Not really. And there were very few people I connected with in general, even out of the people I knew well. Austin was one of the few people who I would open up to.

The women... no thank you.

But of course, there had been *her*.

Isabelle.

God, that had been more than five years ago, before I'd left for business school. And the night had been just like all the others—find a pretty girl, take her home for the night, have a good fuck, and she was gone by morning.

Except, it hadn't been like the others at all. I'd had a connection with her in a way I'd never had with anyone. It had been perfect in so many ways.

But she was the one woman whose number *wasn't* in my phone. The one person I would have liked to call to ask her to join me at the party.

What the hell was I thinking? She was just another woman I'd fucked. And the more I'd thought about that night without finding her, the more fictional the whole thing had become. I'd probably turned her into the perfect woman in my mind, and the only reason she stayed that way was because I couldn't find her. We hadn't spent enough time together for her to prove me wrong about her.

That was how it usually worked. Women were all the same, weren't they?

They all ended up wanting something from me. Whether it was a piece of my business, some of my money, or to wriggle into a part of me that I kept shut to everyone, only so that they could use it to manipulate me.

It was probably better that I didn't see Isabelle again, because as long as I didn't, she remained perfect.

I finally forced myself to text Mia, the best of the women I'd been with if I had to compare notes. She was a blonde bombshell but she had an okay head on her shoulders—she was smarter than she liked to admit—and she was easy enough to turn down if I had to. Some of them put up so much of a fight when I wanted to send them home, and I wasn't ready for the drama.

Beth got back to me with times and arrangements just after I arrived at the hotel.

I had two hours to catch up on sleep, and then it was time to get going again.

After my nap, I dressed in a tuxedo. Austin and I left the hotel together, riding in the black car that we were being chauffeured around in while we were in LA. The car stopped in front of the Glasshouse, and we climbed out.

The restaurant was almost entirely made up of glass

windows that looked out over spectacular sea views on the one end and toward downtown LA on the other. Music thumped over invisible speakers and men and women wearing evening attire moved around to the beat of the music or toward each other, feeding off the excitement in the air.

"This is it," Austin said, clapping me on the back. "Let's get in there and celebrate!"

I smiled and nodded, following my friend into the building.

It was good to be around so many people I knew, so many people who were happy for us and willing to share in our victory.

Mia arrived at one point, found me, and hung on my arm for the rest of the night. She was gracious and sweet and she made it seem like it hadn't been a bad idea to invite her out.

We drank. We partied. We ate good food.

We celebrated a lot of hard work paying off, and a company whose future looked brighter every moment.

There was still a long road to walk, but things were definitely turning out right. I was the luckiest man on Earth, and even though I was far from being the wealthiest, if things continued the way they were now, I was going to get there someday.

I should have been happy. Ecstatic, even. Everything was working out. There was no reason to be down in the dumps about anything.

And yet, something was missing. Something felt wrong. It was great that the business was doing so well, but I'd thought after so much work and such a big payoff, I would have felt more fulfilled. Instead, I felt like I was looking at the crowd as if I wasn't a part of it. I looked at the partygoers, I heard their laughter, and I felt removed.

When I saw Austin, I knew that I should have looked the same—happy, successful, proud.

I just didn't *feel* that way.

I wanted to share something like this with someone who really mattered. It was great that Austin wanted to shout it from the rooftops, and wanted to host the party, but I wanted to be able to call someone very close to me and say, "Hey, I made it."

My mom had been gone for years. All of this was for her, and there wasn't a day I didn't wish she could have seen it.

But I wanted something else, too. *Someone* else. I wanted to be able to go home to someone at the end of the day and fall wearily into their arms. I wanted to be able to share the good news with someone who would understand what it all meant.

No one here understood what it had taken for me to get here. Not even Austin, not completely.

My mind jumped to Isabelle again. *Izzy.* Would she have understood? Would she have known what it was like for me to achieve this?

There was no point in wondering, because she was the one who'd gotten away.

Austin came to find me.

"Come on, man, you're not partying hard enough." He grabbed a flute of champagne from a passing tray and pressed it into my hand. "You have so much to celebrate, look alive!"

He was right, I did have a lot to celebrate. So, I plastered a smile on my face and tried to enjoy the party.

CHAPTER 7

ISABELLE

I drove back from the restaurant, pushing my car far over the speed limit. I didn't have the cash to cover a fine if I got one, but I was late to pick Liam up from my mom's house.

My shift at the restaurant had gone on longer than it should have—a couple celebrating their first wedding anniversary had stayed forever, and I hadn't been able to leave until they did.

Silently, I cursed people who had no compassion for those of us in the service industry. They could have taken it home, and stared into each other's eyes there.

I was in a bad mood, I was tired, and my day wasn't over yet.

When I pulled into the driveway at my mom's place, tires squealing, she opened the front door.

"I'm so sorry," I said, running up the steps to the front door. "I had a table that just wouldn't leave."

"It's okay, honey," my mom said, hugging me at the door. "You can relax. He's asleep, it's not any extra work for him to sleep here an hour or two later."

I shook my head. "But it's still not right. God, I feel like I'm dropping the ball on everything."

My mom followed me into her house.

"You're too hard on yourself," she said. "You're doing great."

I nodded, hearing her words, but I didn't believe them.

I walked into the second bedroom, which used to be my old room, and my heart constricted when I saw Liam asleep in bed, curled up in a little ball, sucking his thumb.

He had a head of dark, wild hair just like his father, and sometimes—especially when he was asleep—I was struck by how much he looked like Carter.

I shook off the thought and walked to the bed.

"Come on, sweetheart," I said, hoisting him into my arms. He mumbled something in his sleep and flopped over my shoulder.

My mom followed with his bag of toys.

I loaded him into the car-seat and covered him with a blanket. He slept right through it. My mom put his bag into the car next to him, and I quietly shut the door.

"Thank you for everything," I said when I turned to her, the way I did every time she took care of him when I needed to take a shift at the restaurant.

"I'm always here when you need me, honey," my mom said.

I hugged her, and felt tears prick my eyes, but I swallowed them down. I wasn't going to cry. I was just tired.

"I'll call you tomorrow," I said.

I climbed in behind the wheel and drove the short distance to my apartment.

After getting Liam inside and tucked into bed, I walked to my bedroom, where I opened my laptop. I climbed into bed with it, propped myself up against a bunch of pillows, and started working.

I had three graphic design projects for different clients I was trying to juggle to cover the cost of everything my waitress job wouldn't cover. Freelancing was a bitch—I already worked long hours and the time constraints were crazy sometimes. But I had to do it.

There just wasn't any other way.

Liam was the light of my life. He was turning five in a few months. I wanted to get him something nice for his birthday but I wasn't sure I would have enough cash for it.

That made me want to cry all over again.

When I'd learned I was pregnant, I'd recovered after the shock and told myself that no matter what, I was going to make this work.

I'd had the baby, and with the help of my mom, June, and Bernie, I'd managed to get my life on a track that worked with having a baby.

Well, sort of worked.

I quit school, dropping out with a year to go. There was no way I could handle classes while being a single mom and working full-time. My new responsibilities left me no time for making art, so eventually I'd packed away my oil paints and brushes. I took a quick graphic design course, and started doing odd jobs wherever I could—online and in restaurants—to cover the bills.

It had been hard. It still was.

But whenever I looked at Liam, I knew it was worth it. He was everything that meant anything to me, and I wasn't going to give up fighting for him. He deserved a good life, and I worked my fingers to the bone to give it to him.

As I worked on the project, touching up colors, arranging texts, I started thinking about the long run. Right now, this was okay. I was working two jobs, I was getting by, and with a little help, I could even get more than four hours' sleep a night sometimes.

But I knew I wasn't going to be able to do this forever. The older Liam got, the more things I wanted to be able to give him, and do for him.

Money was very tight as it was, and I knew this lifestyle wasn't sustainable. I wasn't going to be able to keep doing this and make it through. I didn't sleep enough, and I often forgot to eat. Worst of all, I didn't get to spend enough time with my son.

I was going to have to do something different. I was going to need to find something else, something with solid hours so that I could arrange for a regular sitter instead of relying on my mom and my friends. A job that paid better than the measly income I made each week on waitressing shifts and the bit of cash my freelancing brought me.

I needed something solid.

I finally finished my graphic design jobs for the night. My head hurt, and my eyes felt gritty, but I had one last thing I wanted to do before I went to bed.

I needed to send in applications for a new job.

I started searching the web, reading classifieds, saving those that might work. When I'd collected a few of them, I started sending my resume. I emailed them one by one, and as I did, I sent a silent cry for help, hoping beyond hope that something would come of it. I had no qualifications, aside from the course I'd done, and my experience in anything other than graphic design and waitressing was minimal.

But something had to give, right? My life couldn't be like this forever.

Finally, when there was no more I could do tonight, I clicked off the light and wriggled beneath the sheets. I closed my eyes and tried to relax my aching muscles, tried to switch off my weary mind.

Slowly, as I started drifting off to sleep, I started thinking about things other than the money I needed to make to keep a roof over our heads and food in our bellies.

Carter flashed in my mind. Dark hair, and those piercing eyes. His charming, easy smile.

What would my life have been like if I'd been able to find him after that night? What would have happened if he'd known about Liam? Would we be together? Maybe… maybe not. But at least he would have helped me out financially, if nothing else.

God, what I would have given to have someone who could ease the burden just a little. Sometimes, I had nothing left to give, and I wished that things had been different.

And what if things had worked out between us? What if we'd fallen in love?

Carter's eyes, intense and deep, staring at mine, flashed before me once more.

I pushed the thought of him out of my mind. Thinking about him was no use. I just had to hope that one of those applications I'd sent in would make a difference, and things would start looking up for us.

I had to believe that was how it was going to work, because the alternative wasn't something I was willing to accept.

When I woke up the next morning, Liam sat on my bed, staring at me.

His big brown eyes were filled with laughter, and his face had a mischievous expression.

"You're awake, big boy," I said, reaching for him.

"I've been awake forever," he said.

"That's an incredibly long time to be awake," I said.

"I *know*." He clambered over me and wriggled underneath the sheets. I pulled him tightly against me and cuddled him as long as he let me before he started squirming.

"What's for breakfast, Mommy?" he asked.

I glanced at the time. I had a few hours before I had to be at the restaurant again.

"Let's make pancakes," I said.

"Yay! Pancakes!"

He jumped out of bed and ran out of the room. I laughed and got out of bed. I wrapped a robe around my shoulders and followed Liam to the cramped little kitchen where he was already rummaging for pans under the sink.

"Hey, one step at a time," I said. "Do you remember what we need?"

"A pan," Liam said gravely. "And the pancakes."

I laughed. "You're right. But let's start with flour and eggs and sugar."

Liam nodded and I told him where to get everything while I started putting our breakfast together.

Now that it was the light of a new day, I felt better about everything. My life was still complicated, I still had a lot of work—nothing had magically changed since last night. But a good night's sleep and a bit of sunshine made everything seem more bearable. I didn't know how yet, but we were going to be okay.

"Can I go to Noah's house?" Liam asked.

"Noah?"

"Yeah, Mommy. From playgroup." He rolled his eyes.

"Right." Of course I knew his friend Noah. But my brain had been in a state of overwhelm for so long, sometimes it took me a moment to remember details.

I'd planned to take Liam to my mom's place while I worked today. But if Charlene, Noah's mom, was free for a playdate, maybe I could give Liam a good time and my mom a break all in one go.

"I'll call Noah's mom and let you know what she says, okay?"

Liam nodded, and we made pancakes together. He helped

53

me mix the batter, and when I started cooking them on the stove, he built a fortress on the table out of the Legos my mom had gotten him for Christmas. When one of the pancakes was ready and cool enough to eat, I put it on a plate for him. He left his Legos alone long enough to gobble it up.

I nibbled the pancakes as well, eating as I cooked.

Our bellies were soon full, and it was time to get dressed.

We went through the motions and no matter what we did, Liam had me laughing and smiling. He was always in a good mood, always ready for a laugh, and he was inquisitive as hell. Whenever I spent time with him, I was reminded that this was what it was all for. And then it became more and more bearable.

After getting Liam in front of a kids' TV show, I hopped into the shower, leaving the door open a crack so I could hear if he called me. I showered in record time, and when I was ready, I called Charlene.

She was more than happy to take Liam while I was at work, and I breathed a sigh of relief. I knew my mom needed to catch up on other things in her life for once.

I was on the way to Charlene's to drop Liam off before my shift when I got a call.

"Is this Isabelle Taylor?"

I confirmed that I was.

"I'm calling in regard to a resume we received from you." My ears started ringing. Liam sang something in the car-seat behind me, and I had to focus on the road. "Will you be able come in for an interview this afternoon?"

"Yes!" I cried out. I would figure something out with my work shift. I would take my lunch hour early, or late, or whenever, so that I could go. "I'll be there. You just say when and I'm there."

The voice on the other end of the line chuckled before giving me a time.

"I'll see you then," she said, and a moment later, the call ended.

"Oh, my gosh," I breathed.

"Oh, my gosh," Liam echoed.

I glanced at him in the rearview mirror. "If we're lucky, baby, everything's going to change."

He carried on singing his song, and I carried on driving, almost too nervous to hope.

CHAPTER 8

CARTER

"If we work on Chicago and Miami first, we're going to hit the ground running," Austin said.

We stood in the foyer of our building, talking. Since the party, he hadn't been able to shut up about the new franchises. I was glad he was so eager to get started. It was always a good thing to have people on board who were passionate about what they were doing. And Austin was about as passionate as they came.

I was just as serious about the job, but lately, I'd been feeling distracted. I loved running Appetite, and I was lucky that my mom's dream also turned out to be so profitable. Even if it hadn't been, I wouldn't have stopped doing it.

The money was a silver lining.

But even with everything working out the way it was supposed to, I felt like something was missing.

"I think you know exactly where we should start," I said. "If you get the campaigns up and running, we'll focus on Miami, and do Chicago next."

Austin nodded, excited. "I'm on it. We're going to seal this deal before month-end if what I'm planning works out."

I laughed and clapped my friend on the back. I was lucky to be able to work with my best friend. It didn't often work to do business as friends—I'd seen a lot of friendships fall apart because of work. But Austin was as driven and serious as I was, and that helped a lot.

I was about to say something else to Austin when something caught my eye. A flash of red—it was just for a moment, but my heart stopped.

I craned my neck to see what it was, but I couldn't find it.

When I stepped away from Austin, I heard him ask me something, but I couldn't focus on his words. I couldn't think straight.

I had to be sure…

There.

She walked across the lobby, heading toward the reception desk. Her hair was just as fiery as when I'd seen her the first time.

It was *her.*

Isabelle.

Izzy.

And she was here. In my building.

I couldn't stop staring at her. She wore black pants and a white button-up shirt, her hair twisted into a bun, but there was no way that was going to tame the red wildfire that was her hair.

She'd grown up. Her body was curvier than before, and she'd changed. If it was possible, she'd become more beautiful. Irresistible.

Her face was thinner though, and she looked a bit tired. But her big brown eyes were as bright and beautiful as I remembered them.

What was she doing here?

For a moment, I was at a loss. She couldn't be here for me. She had no idea I was here in LA. Much less in this building.

Suddenly, I remembered the job postings. She had to be here for an interview.

"Austin," I said, tugging at his sleeve until he paid attention. "What jobs do we have open right now?"

"Graphic designer," he said immediately. "For those campaigns we were just talking about."

"Right," I said.

Graphic designer. And she was an artist. She'd had paint all over her hands that night. Back then, she'd been studying something she was passionate about, even though it went against the grain. Even though making a living would be hard. Switching to graphic design seemed sensible.

"Do we know anything about the interviews?" I asked Austin.

"Yeah," Austin said. "I'm talking to HR about it."

"I want a list," I said.

"What?"

I looked at Austin, finally tearing my eyes away from Isabelle.

"I want a list of all the applicants. I want to be involved in the process."

"Why?" Austin asked. "You do the food and the finances. I handle this."

"I know," I said. "But I want to know what's going on with the campaigns, too."

Austin nodded. "Okay, I'll send you the list. But you're going to be bored out of your mind before long."

I nodded. "That's fine."

I knew I wasn't going to be bored out of my mind if Izzy had anything to do with it. I wanted to see her again. I *needed* to see her again. And this was the way I was going to be able to do it. If I got that list, I would finally be able to find her.

If she was here, she needed a job. And that was fine,

because it turned out I had a job she could do. If that was what she was here for, I would give her what she needed.

I would make sure she was the one they hired for the position.

"Earth to Carter," Austin said, and I realized he'd still been talking to me. "I'm saying that the list shouldn't be too long by the end of the day, they should have shortlisted a few already."

I shook my head. "I want the whole list."

Austin groaned. "You can be such a pain in the ass, man. And without warning."

I grinned at Austin. "Just get me that list."

Austin grumbled something else, but told me he would do it, and that was all I cared about. I was going to pull some strings and make this work.

When I looked up at Isabelle again, she was in the elevator. I caught one last look at her before the doors closed.

I stared at the elevator in a daze for a long moment after she'd left.

"Okay, I'm headed up," Austin said.

"Up?"

"To do the interviews," Austin said, looking at me like I'd lost my mind.

"*You're* doing them? Yourself?"

Austin laughed. "Sometimes I think you don't know what I do in this company. Yeah, *I'm* doing them. Myself. I like being a part of the process, vetting them to be sure we get the right ones on board. You're the one always striving for excellence and you pay me a hell of a lot of money, so you best know I'm going to give you excellence."

I snorted. Excellence was all well and good. But right now, the only thing I cared about was in that elevator, riding her way up to the interview that was going to change her life. *My* life.

"Isabelle," I said, grabbing Austin's arm when he started walking away.

"Who?"

"Isabelle. She'll be on your list. Hire her."

"Okay…" he hesitated. "Right away? Without going through the process?"

"Right away."

"And the rest of them?"

"Tell them the position's been filled."

Austin narrowed his eyes at me. "What's gotten into you? What if she's no good?"

"Then I'll handle it." I was sure Isabelle would be good. She would be better than good. She was *perfect.*

It's just the Isabelle in your mind, I reminded myself. It was hard to find flaws in the memory of a woman who had rocked my world for long enough that I would never forget it, and disappeared before she could show me any downfalls of knowing her. But I wanted another taste. I wanted to see her again.

I knew it would burst the bubble I had of her. No one was perfect. That was why I never dated, why I didn't settle down with anyone. I liked the bubble, the dream. And I didn't like getting to know someone that would end up being less than perfect.

With Isabelle, it was different. I wanted to see her again, bursting bubble be damned. I knew she couldn't be perfect. But to me, she still was.

"Let me know when you're talking to her," I said.

Austin nodded, wriggled free of my grip, and proceeded to the elevator. I stared at him just long enough to see him shaking his head.

Was I acting like a fool? Absolutely. But Izzy had driven me crazy the night I'd met her. And now, over five years later, she was still driving me crazy. I needed her to work here. I had to have her around me.

I needed Austin to make it work.

Otherwise, I would walk in there and hand her the job myself.

CHAPTER 9

ISABELLE

$\mathcal{I}$ swallowed hard and tried not to squirm in my seat. I'd slipped away from work, telling my manager I needed to run to the store for something, and my time was running out. The man opposite me seemed more interested in his phone than in me.

"Mr. Shannon?" I asked.

He glanced up at me from his phone.

"Is there anything else you would like to ask me?"

"Yeah," he said, but he didn't put the phone down. "Tell me about yourself."

"Oh," I said. "Well, I'm an artist at heart, and I believe my passion for creativity will shine through in all my work here. I'm someone who understands dedication and commitment. I understand going the extra mile and working for long-term goals, but I also focus on the details of the here and now because they're just as important."

Austin Shannon made an "mm-hmm" sound as I talked. I got the feeling he wasn't really paying attention.

God, it wasn't going well at all, was it? I was nervous.

No, I was downright panicked.

It was the first time in a long time I had no idea if anything was going to work out. Until now, I'd been determined to make it work, no matter what. And despite obstacles, I'd managed to land on my feet every time.

Like a cat.

I held onto that idea as if it was a lifeline. No matter what happened in this interview, I was going to make it through.

I always did.

Besides, Liam needed me to make it. I had to make ends meet for him, to give him the life he deserved.

Mr. Shannon didn't ask me more questions. He typed on his phone with a grin, and looked like he'd forgotten I was here at all. My heart sank.

I wasn't going to get this job, was I?

I'd been so happy when they'd called me this morning, asking me to come in for an interview right away. I'd sent out a bunch of resumes in a panic and it had been like a lifeline, something that had appeared from the darkness to pull me up and save me from drowning in my mess. It wasn't my ideal job, but it would be stable hours, better pay, and I would be able to give Liam some stability and my poor mother a break.

Maybe I could even afford daycare if I was careful with my money.

But it turned out not to have been the answer to my prayers after all. It had been a false alarm. It was obvious by how my interviewer was totally blowing me off.

I glanced at my wristwatch. If I didn't get going, I was going to lose my job at the restaurant. I couldn't afford my bills if I had to rely on my freelance jobs alone.

"If that's all, Mr. Shannon," I started, not able to hide the irritation from my voice. "I won't waste any more of your time."

He blinked at me, surprised. "You're leaving?"

I nodded. "It seems this interview is over." *If it really started,* I added mentally.

His phone beeped again, and I didn't hide the roll of my eyes.

"Miss Taylor," he said, looking up at me. "It looks like you're the perfect candidate."

I frowned at him. "What?"

"Your resume is impressive, you're clearly passionate about what you do, and... I'd like to offer you the job."

My jaw dropped and I gaped at him, not trying to hide my confusion.

"I don't understand."

Mr. Shannon pushed his hands into his pockets casually. "I've been authorized to hire you right away if you'll accept the offer. So, what do you say, Miss Taylor? How do you feel about being our new in-house campaign designer?"

I had no idea how this had just happened. Was he... offering me the job? Without a vague 'I'll call you back,' or a second round of interviews, or... anything?

"Miss Taylor?" Mr. Shannon prompted.

"Oh, my God. Yes!" I exclaimed. "I mean, of course." I barked a laugh I couldn't contain before I clasped my fingers over my lips. "Where do I sign?"

Mr. Shannon chuckled. "We'll take care of the paperwork when you come into work on Monday."

"Monday?"

"Is that too soon?" he asked, looking concerned.

I shook my head. "Not at all. I'll be here first thing."

His concern melted into a satisfied grin and he opened the office door for me so that I could walk out. I contained myself beautifully. I kept my composure.

"If you have a bit of time, I'd like to give you a tour of the facilities," he said when I wanted to turn toward the elevator.

I glanced at my wristwatch again. If I didn't leave right

this minute, I was going to be done at the restaurant for sure. But… I had a job! A great one! For the first time, I could close my eyes and jump without worrying that Liam would be without a safety net too.

"Of course," I said. "I just need to make a quick call."

Mr. Shannon nodded and I took out my phone, dialing my manager's number to tell him something came up and I couldn't finish my shift.

Something came up all right, but I couldn't work the rest of the month—or the rest of my *life*—in that hellhole.

When I ended the call, the weight fell off my shoulders and I took a deep breath, letting it out slowly.

"Ready?" Mr. Shannon asked.

I nodded and plastered a professional smile on my face, even though on the inside, I was bubbling and burning with the desire to call my mom, to call my friends, to shout it out to the world that *finally* something was going my way.

Mr. Shannon seemed a lot more present and engaged when he took me through the building. He showed me everything there was to see in the place. The different departments where people in neat clothing were hard at work. The cafeteria where he said they even catered for vegetarians, food allergies, and various religious diets. The garden outside where stressed workers could take a break and enjoy the fresh air, and so much more.

I struggled to take it all in. I only partially absorbed the loads of information he was dumping on me about the company. It was a large gourmet food distributor, and he talked rapidly about how food evoked emotion. He wanted me to bring that out in the campaign he was planning.

My heart was singing. All I could think about was Liam's face and how it lit up whenever he saw me, and how I'd be able to see it even more now. I'd finally be able to spend more time with my son. We wouldn't have to scrape by, and

I wouldn't be consumed by stress. It was a dream come true.

We rode the elevator to one of the top floors, where Mr. Shannon wanted to introduce me to the head of human resources. She was going to take care of my contract and account details on Monday, so it would be good for me to know her.

This part of the building was slick and luxurious, with thick carpets underfoot, rich wallpaper, and heavy bookcases along some of the walls. The people who passed us were dressed even more sharply than the rest of the staff, and they looked clean and polished and sure of themselves. It was clear I was in the management part of the company. The place had an air of reverence.

The conference rooms had large glass partitions rather than walls, and we walked past a meeting in session.

When I glanced at the man who stood at the end of the long table, my heart stopped.

I knew that face. The dark hair, the piercing eyes, the way his mouth moved when he talked.

I was jerked from the present and thrown back in time, to a place where a handsome college graduate had bought me a drink late at night and taken me back to his apartment. I was suddenly back in college, sleeping with the one man who had managed to see me for who I really was.

Carter.

The father of my child.

"Are you coming?" Mr. Shannon asked, and I realized I'd fallen behind. I nodded and hurried to catch up to him, but my eyes drifted back to Carter where he stood in front of a group of people, in command, in control, completely at ease.

At the last moment before I passed, his eyes locked on mine.

And he smiled.

He wasn't shocked to see me. He wasn't as shaken as I was. The look on his face seemed *normal.* He seemed like he'd expected to see me standing in the hall, gaping at him.

My blood rushed in my ears and I felt hot. My button-up shirt suddenly felt like it was choking me. I tugged at the collar.

"Here we are," Mr. Shannon said. He knocked on an office door before pushing it open. "Hannah," he said with a smile.

A blonde woman with a short bob and straight bangs stood and smiled.

"Austin," she said. "What can I do for you?"

"This is Isabelle Taylor," he said, beckoning for me to join them. "She's starting work here on Monday, and she'll come to you first thing in the morning. Isabelle, this is Hannah Fleming, Director of HR. She can be your best friend or your worst nightmare, depending on how you conduct yourself."

I swallowed. I was still shaky on my feet with the shock of seeing Carter. With the shock of Carter *not* being shocked at seeing me.

"It's nice to meet you," I said, shaking Hannah's hand.

"Welcome to Appetite, Isabelle," Hannah said. "You'll find that working with us isn't just a job. We're like a family, and we look out for each other."

I smiled. It sounded wonderful. Everything about being here was wonderful. And bizarre.

Hannah and Austin made quick conversation about something that went over my head, then she said, "I'll see you on Monday."

Austin ushered me out of the office again and accompanied me to the lobby. While we walked, he chatted excitedly about the campaign we would work on. I tried to focus on what he was saying—I had to take all of this in. This was my foreseeable future. But I couldn't stop thinking about Carter, about what he'd looked like when I saw him, and about the fact that *somehow* he'd known I was here.

Why was he here? I'd thought he'd left LA. And after all this time, all the wishing I could find him and tell him about our son, now I'd be *working* with him?

God, my mind spun.

"I look forward to working together, Isabelle," Austin said when we stepped out of the elevator in the lobby.

"Thank you, Mr. Shannon," I said, shaking his hand one more time. "For everything. I look forward to it, too. I'll see you on Monday."

He turned around and walked away, and I left the building. I walked to my car and climbed behind the wheel. I hurried, turning the key in the ignition while pulling my seatbelt on in a frenzy. As was my habit. Then realized I had nowhere to rush to. I could take a moment and breathe.

I did just that. I took a deep breath in, and let it out again. In. Out.

When I put my car into gear, I turned it toward home. I could spend time with my boy. I could give my mom a break.

And I could tell them that, for the first time, our luck was going to change.

After locking eyes with Carter, I had a feeling that a *lot* of things were about to change.

CHAPTER 10

CARTER

*I*t took me over five years to get her off my mind. Five years where she would show up in my dreams unannounced and fuck up my day. Five years where I would work hard, powering on, and suddenly I would flash on her face and it would floor me.

After so long, I thought I'd gotten my strange Isabelle addiction out of my system.

Until the moment I saw her again.

It was as if everything had come back into focus again. As if I'd walked through life with everything around me a blur, and suddenly with her in it, the image was crystal clear.

And now, she was right here, under my nose where I could keep an eye on her.

"She was rattled as fuck, man," Austin said when he sat on my desk in my office, swinging his legs like a kid. "She thought I wasn't paying any attention to her. First, there were your constant texts. Then I had to look at her portfolio on the spot to make sure she wasn't incompetent. I was a little distracted. She was ready to leave."

"You made her stay, and that's what counts," I said, looking out through the window.

"What is it with this one, anyway?" Austin asked. "Since when do you get your balls in a twist over a woman?"

I shrugged. Austin was right, I didn't usually get worked up over any particular woman. I seduced them, I fucked them, I sent them on their way. That was what Carter Jacobs did. I didn't commit, I didn't call back, I didn't do second dates or second chances.

They didn't work for me.

But with Isabelle, it was different. *She* was different. She had been from the moment I'd seen her working behind the counter at that little café close to the college I'd graduated from. She'd been spectacular, taking my breath away with how incredibly raw and natural and unapologetically authentic she was. And then she'd blown my mind with the best, most incredible, most *personal* sex I'd ever had with a stranger.

And then, just as I'd thought I found the one girl that would change my mind about everything—about my damn life itself—I woke up to an empty bed.

But she was here now, and she wasn't slipping through my fingers again. I had her number. I had her address. And she worked for me.

Well, not directly.

But that was going to change. Austin thought he had it all figured out—she was a good designer, as luck would have it. After looking at her portfolio, he'd been impressed by her work. She'd be an asset to the company, he assured me. She was going to blow up his campaign. He was sure of it. He was excited.

But there was no way in hell I was letting Isabelle work for him. I wasn't going to stand having her in my company when she wasn't working directly for me.

I knew I would be breaking all kinds of protocols, but I was the boss. I could do whatever the fuck I wanted.

And I wanted her working under me.

I cocked a grin at the thought.

I wanted her under me for other purposes, too.

When I closed my eyes, I could still hear her moans in my ear. I could still see the red flash of hair in the near dark as she bucked and curled and writhed against me. I could still taste her skin on my lips.

All in good time, though. All in good time.

I'd gotten through the past several years without her. If I'd been able to wait that long, I could wait a little more.

"Cynthia?" I called, and my secretary popped her head around my office door. "Set up a meeting with Derek Grimes."

"When?"

"As soon as he's available. Before the weekend."

She nodded and disappeared.

"What do you need to talk to Derek for?" Austin asked.

Grimes was the design director at the company. He worked directly under Austin, and technically Isabelle was his new hire.

Not that I gave a shit about that. I was going to poach her no matter where her position suggested she should be. But I had to talk to Derek about it. He was going to be pissed if I just took her without explaining to him why. He was going to be sour that he would have to find another designer just when he thought we'd solved his problem.

That was up to Austin to clear up, though. Not that I was going to tell Austin that. Not yet. I was going to keep it all to myself until I had her under *me*.

I relished the possibilities of what that could mean.

"What's on your mind, Carter?" Austin asked, his voice driving through my thoughts. "You're being weird."

"How?" I asked, turning to face him.

Austin shrugged. "I don't know. You're more full of shit than usual. And this silent treatment thing you've been doing all day—"

"I'm not giving you the silent treatment," I laughed.

"Yeah, well, you're not telling me what's going on, and that's the same thing," Austin said.

"Aww, don't pout," I mocked and he flipped me off before he laughed.

I laughed, too. I would tell Austin what was going on eventually. For now, though, I needed to figure out what I was feeling. I knew I felt *something* when I was with Isabelle. Something… different. Not just lust, like I usually did. But I'd pushed that feeling away five years ago and I was shocked at the strength with which it returned today. It was as if seeing her made everything I'd done fall into place. Like she was the last piece to the puzzle.

And I wasn't sure how that was possible with a woman I'd only slept with one night.

When I'd slept with so many of them and barely remembered them at all.

On Monday morning, I was at the office just after seven. It was early—so much earlier than I usually came in. But I wanted to meet her. I wanted to talk to her, personally.

I wanted to be the one to escort her into the building.

When she arrived, she took my breath away. Her hair was bright red, flaming in the early morning sun. She wore tailored black pants and a crisp white button-up shirt, and the stark color scheme made her red hair and bright eyes stand out that much more.

"Carter," she said when she met me in the lobby. She didn't look nearly as shocked to see me as she'd looked the day we'd hired her, when she'd passed the conference room.

I'd relished her surprise then. I was drawn to her cool confidence now.

"How are you, Isabelle?" I asked. I fought the urge to reach for her, to pull her closer to me and breathe in the smell of her shampoo.

"A little overwhelmed," she admitted. "But ready to make a difference in the company."

"My company," I said.

She hesitated a moment, realization dawning on her, and then she smiled. Her smile spread across her face, slowly and beautifully, like a sunrise, and lit up her features.

"Of course," she breathed.

"Come," I said. "I'm in charge of showing you to your desk."

She nodded, and we walked to the elevator together. When the doors slid closed, I was hyper-aware of her standing next to me. The elevator was small, the space pushing us closer together. I studied her features, staring unashamedly. Her porcelain skin was smooth, her hair seemed to be the same deep red I remembered, and she carried herself with fluid grace, standing upright and confident next to me.

She glanced at me when I wouldn't stop staring. Her cheeks pinkened.

"What?" she asked.

"It's just… crazy. That you're here," I said.

God, could I sound like more of an idiot?

"Yeah," she said. "Crazy."

The atmosphere shifted a little and I wanted to say something else. Something personal. Like, that it was amazing seeing her again. Or that she looked incredible. Or that the past five years had been empty, hollow, and for the first time I felt like maybe this was why.

The elevator pinged and the doors slid open before I could do something stupid. We stepped out.

Isabelle's new office was on my floor. It wasn't protocol for new employees to start up on the top floor, but I didn't care. I wanted her close by, where I could see her.

"This is… nice," she said when we walked into her office. "*Really* nice."

I smiled and watched her as she turned around, taking it all in. The office was big, with a beautiful view of the city and a splash of the ocean on the horizon. Her furniture was new, and I'd left a catalog on her desk so she could choose decorations and ornaments and paintings, or whatever her heart desired to make the space personal to her.

"I know Austin hired you to work on a campaign, but there's been a change of plans. I'm going to need you to help me with a new product line launch."

She blinked at me. "A what?"

"I'm launching a new product line and it needs to be ready to get out there in as little time as possible. We're talking all the way through from conceptual designs to marketing."

She shook her head, paling a little. "I can't do that. I'm not qualified to oversee something like a launch. I was a free-lance graphic designer, Carter. I didn't even finish my degree."

I frowned. I'd known she hadn't finished her degree—I'd pored over her file when Austin had given it to me. But the way she said it, the look on her face, suggested something had happened.

"Why not?" I asked before I could think about it. What had changed her life so drastically, when before she had been such a dedicated student, such a good girl?

Her jaw tightened and her body language changed. Closed off. Damn it, it hadn't been my place to ask.

"Life happens, you know?" she answered. Vague, but she wasn't pushing me away.

"I know," I said, nodding.

She shook her head slightly and glanced at her desk. "I can try to do all of this for you, but I have no idea where to start." I liked that she was admitting to her shortcomings.

"I'll help you," I said.

She nodded and walked to her desk. She sat down and flattened her hands on the surface, looking up at me. Her smile was bright and glowing when she flashed it again.

"I didn't think this was where I would end up."

Again, I wanted to ask more questions about what her life had been like for the past five years, but I bit my tongue this time.

"I'll send you the files in a moment," I said. "Get comfortable in your office, and then go to see Hannah. When you're ready, we'll get moving."

She nodded and I left her office, forcing myself to walk away.

Isabelle was back in my life. I struggled to wrap my mind around it. And this time, she wasn't going anywhere. She'd been almost a figment of my imagination for so long, someone I dreamed about, someone that didn't exist in my life anymore, that it was hard to think that this was real.

But it was. She was in the office just down the hall from mine. And even though she was terrified of the project—I was throwing her into the deep end in a big way—she hadn't turned it down.

I was looking forward to working with her.

One thing I knew for sure—I was screwed. I'd believed she was perfect all these years. I expected to have a hard crash back to reality as soon as I got to know her, because there wasn't a perfect woman out there.

What if she turned out to be just like the rest of them?

But now that I'd been around her, and she'd admitted that she hadn't finished her degree, that she wasn't qualified for her job, and I'd seen her nervous and panicked under her composed mask, I just liked her more for her flaws.

CHAPTER 11

ISABELLE

I was struggling to keep up with how fast everything was changing.

I'd had a few days to get my head straight, to celebrate the new job and arrange normal times for my mom to pick up Liam from preschool and help babysit until I got home from work. But I still felt like I'd been steamrolled.

And Carter... God. I wasn't sure what to do with all the new information that was being dumped on me.

Not only was he hotter than ever—and I remembered him being drop-dead *gorgeous* already—the sexual tension between us was as serious as it had been before.

If not more.

Not only that, he was suddenly my boss. How had that happened? I'd been sure that I would work with Austin Shannon. But Carter had been there to receive me—cue the butterflies—and he'd put me up in an office that looked like it came straight from a movie set.

When I came back from Hannah's office, where we'd taken care of my contract and account details, a young woman was waiting in my office.

"Hi," she said brightly.

She had black hair that had been pulled back from her face, bright green eyes, and a slim, tall body.

"Hi," I said carefully.

"I'm Felicity. I work in design, too. I heard you were new."

I nodded. "Isabelle. Friends call me Izzy."

Felicity grinned a row of perfectly white teeth at me. "Izzy. I like that." She tilted her head to the side a little, studying me. "So, you're the girl he poached from Derek, huh?"

"What?" I asked. I had no idea what she was saying.

"You've got to be some special kind of artist if Jacobs decided to use you for himself."

I blinked. "Carter?"

"Oh, first-name basis. Wow."

I shook my head, squeezing my eyes shut for a moment. "I'm a little lost."

"Don't worry about it, we all feel that way during our first month here at Appetite. Jacobs is a hell of a boss to be working for. But you'll learn as you go along. You just need to jump *before* he snaps his fingers, and you'll stay off his radar."

I frowned. Was she talking about Carter? It didn't sound anything like Carter.

"Come with me, I'll show you the kitchen," Felicity said, looping her arm through mine as if we were best friends. "It's literally the only place you'll really want to know when you get into things here. You can meet the rest of our team, too. Jacobs is having a staff meeting in half an hour, so you get to see him in action."

"Oh," I said. I felt like I was completely out of my depth. "I have to take care of a few things for him first."

Felicity shook her head. "You don't want to miss the staff meeting. When Jacobs calls, you answer."

"What do you mean by that?" I asked.

Felicity snorted and rolled her eyes. "You'll get to know him. He's an asshole."

An asshole? Carter?

We walked into a break room that looked a lot more like an upscale coffee house, complete with a barista station, comfortable couches arranged in a semicircle, a water cooler and a fridge, and a few tables dotted around the rest of the open space. A few employees were seated on the couches and around the tables. Some of them glanced up when we walked in. Some of them leaned forward and gossiped about me, not even hiding the fact that I was the hot topic of conversation around here.

I wanted to crawl away again, but that was no way to deal with this. I was on this team now, and I was going to hold my head up high and fill the shoes Carter had offered me.

Even though I wasn't sure how I was going to do that.

"Everyone," Felicity said, raising her voice. Everyone fell quiet. "This is Izzy. Izzy, this is everyone."

She gestured with her hand. A few of them nodded and waved in response.

"Come on," Felicity said and led me to a coffee station where she started preparing us each a cup. "Do you see that woman over there?" She nodded to a scrawny blonde who looked nervous. "That's Danielle. She's had a crush on Jacobs since, like, forever. But *that's* never going to happen."

"Oh. Why doesn't she stand a chance with him?" I asked. *Please don't say he's married,* I willed.

"Because she's not his type."

"What is his type?" I asked, relief washing through me.

"Slutty," Felicity said.

Blood drained from my face. What was she talking about? Surely not Carter, the one guy who'd been everything *but* a dick to me all those years ago. There had to be some kind of mistake.

The conversation stopped abruptly, and when we looked up, each armed with a cup of coffee now, I realized Carter had walked into the room. His presence filled the space, pushing into the corners, and everyone clearly revered him.

"Thank you for being on time," he said in a clipped voice. "This won't be long. Firstly," he glanced at me. "I want to welcome our newest member, Isabelle Taylor. She's going to be working closely with you on the new launch. If she needs help, you're going to jump to give it to her."

I felt self-conscious for a moment, but Carter powered on to the next point of business.

"The vegan campaign was rotten," he continued. "I don't know what the hell any of you were thinking, but since when are vegans fucking different from the rest of us? The campaign sounded like you were trying to single them out."

"I'm sorry, sir?" a man with mouse-brown hair and a flat face asked, interrupting Carter.

Carter shot him a murderous glance, a look that was very out of place on the face I thought I knew.

And just like that, I realized I didn't know it at all.

"What is it?" Carter snapped.

"Well… the responses to the campaign were very good. The numbers are up since we launched it, and—"

"Do I look like I give a rat's ass about the numbers? I care about how people *feel*, Donovan. This business isn't just about money, it's about emotion. And if we can't evoke the right emotion, we shouldn't be doing this at all. It's your job to make my food look good. Do. Your. Job."

He turned around and stormed out of the break room.

I gasped. "What the hell was that?"

"A staff meeting," Felicity said with a shrug. "This is a good day. You don't want to see him when he's pissed off."

I frowned. I was starting to think I really *didn't* want to see him pissed off.

Where was the Carter I'd met that night? Where was the man I remembered almost every time I looked at my little boy at home? This Carter was an asshole, just like Felicity had said.

"No one seems upset by his outburst," I said, looking at the others who were slowly starting to disperse now that they'd been dismissed by Carter's dramatic exit.

"No point in crying over spilled milk," Felicity said and rolled her eyes. "I hate that saying. But it's true. So, we screwed up. We'll just have to do better this time. There's no pleasing Jacobs, we can only try to do something different next time. We can only hope we'll get it right and he won't piss all over our work. Or fire one of us."

I shook my head. "He sounds terrible."

"He's okay once you get to know him," Felicity said. "Trust me, a lot of women want to know him despite everything he does. And he lets them. I mean, he *knows* them." She winked at me.

My stomach dropped. Women? As in plural?

"Doesn't he date?" I asked, hoping Felicity would say *something* that would redeem him.

She shook her head as we left the break room. "It would be hard to sleep with as many women as he does if he was dating. I mean, a lot of women would jump at the chance to be Mrs. Jacobs. The guy's a millionaire, and he's only thirty. He knows what he's doing, and even though he's not one of the bigshots out there who has so much money he doesn't know what to do with it, he has enough to keep the ladies hungry."

We now reached my office and came to a stop in the doorway.

"So, you're on a first-name basis with him," Felicity said. "How do you know him?"

"Oh," I said, thinking back to that night. To the man I thought he was back then. "We were just acquaintances once upon a time."

"Huh," Felicity said. "Well, you're better off not knowing him more closely, if you catch my drift. Trust me. I'd rather work for him than have his attention in that way. That just ends in disaster." She gave my hand a squeeze. "I'll see you around, girl. Don't hesitate to call me if you need anything at all. I'm just two floors down."

I nodded and watched her go. Felicity walked with a bounce in her step, as if she hadn't just shattered every illusion I had about Carter.

When I'd seen him the other day, standing in the conference room like a commanding captain at the helm of his vessel, it had been a shock. But it had also been an eye-opener. I'd figured out that he was involved with Appetite, and when I Googled it, I'd realize just how involved he truly was.

It had made me think. He had to have been sent across my path again for a reason. I believed in fate, destiny. And in a family that was whole.

Liam deserved to know his father, and one of the first things I'd thought after seeing him was that this was my opportunity to tell Carter about the son he'd never known he had.

But now that Felicity had told me what he was like, I wasn't so sure.

I entered my office and stood there, lost in thought.

Womanizer? Asshole? That wasn't the type of man I wanted in Liam's life. I wanted him to have someone he could look up to, and if what Felicity said about Carter was true, then I wasn't certain I wanted Liam to know who his father was.

Of course, I didn't know which version of Carter was real anymore—the man I'd met five years ago, or the man that Felicity worked for.

It was going to take some time to figure it out.

A knock on my door jerked me out of my spiraling thoughts and Carter stood in front of me.

"Have you had a chance to look at the documents I sent you?" he asked.

I shook my head. "I didn't have time. I'm sorry, I—"

"Don't be. Just get around to it when you have a chance, okay?" He grinned at me and God, it made me weak at the knees. He was a sex god, for lack of a better description. My eyes slid involuntarily to his lips, but I forced them back up.

His eyes were intense, and he grinned at me.

He took a step into my office, closer to me, and his cologne clung to his clothes. I breathed in the scent of him and my body responded with a softening, an opening. My breath caught in my throat.

"You just let me know if there's anything I can do for you," Carter said, coming to a stop right beside me.

I cleared my throat, forcing myself to be professional.

"I will, thank you. I think I should get to work, though."

Carter frowned slightly but his grin stayed in place, and the result made him look mischievous. And kissable.

Fuck.

"I'll let you get to it, then," Carter said. He reached for me, touching his fingers to my elbow. It was a casual gesture, but it felt amazing. Electricity jolted through my body at his touch, and I swallowed hard. "I'll see you around, Izzy. It's good to have you here."

"Thank you," I said and my voice sounded surprisingly calm.

He turned and left the room. I sagged against my desk. Carter's cologne remained for a while after he left, and I struggled to concentrate. I sat behind my desk to go through the documents he'd sent me, but all I could think about was the way his touch had echoed through my body.

Boy, I was in trouble.

CHAPTER 12

CARTER

*I*t'd been a week and I'd been at the office every day. That had to be a new record for me. When I started this whole thing, I'd worked my fingers to the bone, but being the CEO of an established company had its perks. Not having to come in early—or not having to come in at all —was one I used as often as I could.

But this was different. It wasn't that I was more dedicated to my company—although the company was everything to me—it was that I got to see *her*.

Isabelle.

Izzy, as everyone around the office had started to call her.

She was settling in well. She'd made a splash. They all liked her, and I knew why. She was the type of person people gravitated toward, with her positive attitude and her glow. She was nothing like me. I was serious and grumpy and I demanded excellence, which meant I couldn't be friends with the people that worked for me. If I wanted to get to the top and stay there, I had to draw lines I couldn't cross.

And I'd done that. I'd been fine doing it for the longest time.

But seeing her with the others, seeing her fit into the world I'd created with an elegant ease made me... well, it made me fucking *hard.* That was what it did.

Among other things—I envied her for being able to connect with others as easily as she did. I, on the other hand, couldn't seem to make lasting connections.

But I wanted to fuck her. There, I admitted it. She was hot. Beautiful. Funny, kind, smart. And she cared about everyone around her.

And that made me want her as mine. So that she could pour some of that sunshine into my life, too. I wanted to be the center of her attention. There were times when she talked to the others, heads bowed together in deep discussion about the project, and I watched her with a pang of jealousy that that attention wasn't aimed at me.

I thought back to that night in the coffee shop, when we'd sat together in much the same way, and it had been just the two of us wrapped in a bubble with a filmy wall so thin it had burst at the first light of dawn.

"Can I see you in my office?" I asked the next Monday after we'd had a big meeting with the whole crew.

I'd asked her questions in front of the others. I'd asked for her opinion, rather than facts. It had put her on the spot, and she'd blushed so beautifully, I'd wanted to suck on her lips and cup her cheeks. Then her breasts.

I loved watching her squirm, watching her stutter when I spoke to her. I was having fun turning her on. It was punishment for how much she was turning me on without even trying.

And I knew I was getting to her.

When she knocked on my door and stepped in, she looked nervous.

"You wanted to see me?" she asked.

I nodded. "Close the door."

She closed it behind her, and I saw her throat moving as she swallowed.

I stood and walked around my desk so that I stood in front of her. Close.

"Am I in trouble?" she asked.

I shook my head. "No, your work is fantastic."

She let out a breath of relief. "I was afraid you hated what I came up with for the mock-ups. I don't know what I'm doing, not with this. The others are helping me a lot, and—"

"Stop talking," I interrupted her. "I wanted to see you."

"See me about what?" she asked.

I shrugged. "I can't stand being around you without being able to kiss you. And touch you. Without thinking about that night."

"Carter," she said, shaking her head. "You can't talk to me like that. We shouldn't—"

"Who's going to tell Hannah, Izzy?" I asked. "Are you? You can't tell me you don't feel it, too." I reached for her hand and took it. She didn't pull away. Instead, she looked up at me with eyes that were dark with hunger. "I know you want what I want."

"What do you want?" she asked in a breathy voice.

When I leaned in a little, her breath caught in her throat.

"Tell me you want it, too," I said. I pushed my fingers into her hair and stroked her cheek lazily with my thumb. "Or tell me there's nothing here for you, and you don't feel a thing. I'll stop."

"Will you?" she asked. Her voice was just a whisper.

"I will," I said. "But I don't want to."

"I don't want you to," she said, her voice so soft I barely heard it. But she closed her eyes. And I wasn't going to let this opportunity slide. I had to kiss her.

The moment our lips touched, it was like I was yanked

back five years, and I remembered the feel of her, the taste of her, as if it was yesterday that we did this last.

I pulled her tightly against me, wrapping my arms around her body, and she moaned softly at the back of her throat when my tongue slipped into her mouth.

My cock was rock hard in my pants, and I ground my hips against hers. I wasn't going to let this moment stop. I wasn't going to kiss her and then just step away again.

Not like this.

My hands fumbled with the black blouse she wore today, and I pushed my fingers underneath it. I felt her soft skin, and moved up to her chest, cupping her perfect breasts. She gasped and ran her hand through the hair on the back of my head, her nails grazing my scalp and neck as she made her way down. Goosebumps ran down my spine and lust devoured me.

I started pulling her shirt over her head.

"We can't do this," she muttered against my lips. "We're at the office."

"This is my office," I said, walking over to the door to lock it, then returning to her. "My company. I'm going to fuck you on my desk and no one's going to stop me."

"Carter," she said, and I wasn't sure if she was protesting or begging.

"Tell me to stop," I challenged her.

The look on her face was riddled with lust, but I knew she was turning it over in her mind. She was responsible. She'd always looked like the type.

I was responsible, too. But with how fucking turned on I was now, I couldn't be held responsible for anything I was about to do to her. The only thing I wanted held against me was her naked pussy.

I chuckled inwardly at my shitty joke.

She kissed me again and I knew she wanted this as much as I did. She was just as horny for me.

The past week had been torture. Stolen glances, accidental touches, and her body so close to mine whenever we worked together, I could only think about sex.

And then there was the fact that no matter which way I looked at it, she was fucking amazing. There wasn't an inch of her body that wasn't beautiful. She was down to earth and raw and natural and nothing like the bimbos who all tried so damn hard to get my attention that it made them come across as needy or desperate or cunning.

No, Izzy was different.

And that made me want to claim her. Again and again.

So no one else could have her but me.

Her blouse hit the floor, and her pencil skirt followed. I unzipped it in the back with ease and when it slid down her legs, I paused for a moment to take in the glorious sight of her.

A black lace bra and panty set made me want to sit up and beg. Her red hair had come undone from its pins—oops, I'd pushed my hands into her hair too many times—and the wild flames on her shoulders made her look like a vision.

I grabbed her again and kissed her, spinning her around and lifting her onto my desk. She wrapped her legs around my waist and started unbuttoning my shirt. When she'd pushed it off my shoulders, her fingers light on my skin, she started kissing her way down my neck and onto my chest. Her kisses left behind a trail of fire, and my cock strained against my pants, begging to be released so that I could plunge myself into her.

She undid my buckle at the same moment I undid her bra. I pulled it off and dropped it on the floor, and she reached into my pants and pulled out my cock.

"Fuck, I want you so badly," I muttered, kissing her again.

Her fingers worked expertly up and down my cock and my body contracted, my stomach tightening and my balls aching for release.

"So, take me," she responded, and I didn't need to be told twice.

I sank to the floor, peeled her panties down her legs, and dove into her pussy. I licked and sucked her clit so that she gasped and moaned softly, trying to swallow her cries.

I would have loved to feast on her for a long, long time, but we were in the office and chances were someone was going to come looking for me soon. The last thing I wanted was to put her in a bad position just because I didn't want to curb my cock anymore.

So, I stood and pulled my pants down to my thighs, and pulled her closer. At the last moment, I thought about protection—I could be an SOB but let it not be said that I hadn't learned how to be safe these past couple of years. I leaned over the desk, opened the drawer, and took out a condom.

"You keep condoms in your office?" she asked, her face paling a little.

"Yeah." There was no point in hiding who I was. She was getting to know me, so she was going to find out who I was sooner or later.

I ripped the foil and rolled the condom over my cock. When I looked up at her, her eyes were on my cock. Her lips were parted and I would have loved to fuck her mouth first. But time was of the essence. My cock in her mouth would have to wait.

I pushed into her, pulling her against me with her ass on the edge of the desk. She cried out louder than I would have liked. I pressed my fingers against her lips for a moment.

"Hush, sweetheart," I whispered.

I looked her in the eyes when I started pushing into her,

pulling back only to thrust in again, and she moaned and whimpered as I fucked her harder and harder.

Holy shit, she felt *incredible.* I'd had a lot of sex these past few years, but nothing had ever compared to being inside her right now.

And nothing ever would. I was sure of that.

She cried out, quieter this time, and leaned her head on my shoulder, closing her teeth on my skin. She bit down as she orgasmed, and her teeth left marks on my skin.

Fuck, that was so *hot.*

She shuddered and trembled in my arms, her pussy clamping down on my cock. It took everything I had not to orgasm, too.

But I wanted to take her hard and fast from behind, too. I wanted her spread out on my desk, her hair falling over her back.

When I pulled out of her, she whimpered in protest.

I helped her off the desk and she gasped when I spun her around. She leaned forward on the desk, her tits on my year planner, and I pushed shit out of the way to give her space.

Her back was beautiful, long and smooth, and her red hair was in stark contrast to her milky skin. Her ass was perfectly round and delicious, and I grabbed onto her firm cheeks to guide my cock back into her.

She started moaning again when I fucked her from behind. She pressed her mouth against her own arm to muffle her cries, and I gripped her hips, fingers digging into her skin as I plunged into her again and again.

I was going to come, and soon.

"Oh, Carter, fuck!" she bit out, keeping her voice low, and that was what did it.

She pushed me over the edge with three little words.

I plunged into her as deep as I could and released, my cock pounding and throbbing as I emptied my balls into the condom. I gritted my teeth and groaned, and she curled her fingers around the far edge of my desk, holding on as if for dear life.

When the orgasm subsided, I slipped out of her. My cock was already softening.

She straightened up, breathing hard, and looked over her shoulder at me.

If I hadn't just drained my cock, I would have jumped her and fucked her all over again for the sexy look she gave me.

"You should get dressed," I said in a hoarse voice. She nodded, swallowed, and started picking up her clothes from the floor.

I rolled the condom off my cock and disposed of it in my wastebasket. I tugged my pants back up, pulled on my shirt and buttoned up. I tucked it into my pants, fastened the buckle, and it was as if nothing had happened.

A moment later, Izzy was dressed again, and she looked composed as ever, except that her hair hung loose over her shoulders now, instead of pinned up as she'd had it before.

Would anyone notice? Probably not. And if they did, they could keep their judgment to themselves.

"So, like I said," I said with a grin. "You're doing a great job so far."

Her cheeks were flushed and her eyes sparkled. A smile curled around her lips.

"Thank you."

I nodded and she turned, leaving the office. I watched her ass swinging from side to side, and I bit my lip.

My cock was already hardening in my pants, ready for round two.

CHAPTER 13

ISABELLE

I didn't know what I thought was going to happen between me and Carter when I saw him again.

At first, it hadn't been something that would happen at all —he'd gone to New York so soon after we met, and that had been the end of it.

I'd raised Liam on my own, and figured I would keep doing that because I had no idea how to find Carter. I'd never gotten his last name.

When I started the job, I'd decided to hold off on telling him about Liam at first. I wanted to find out more about Carter. I had to make sure he was the type of man I wanted in Liam's life.

Carter deserved to know, and he *would* know. Soon.

But first, I had to know what I was dealing with here. Liam and I had been managing alone for so long. It might be a disruption in my son's life to suddenly bring his dad into his world. I had to figure out how to handle the situation in the best possible way.

So, after almost two weeks of working with Carter, I still hadn't told him about Liam.

We'd slept together in his office just the one time. I probably shouldn't have let that happen, but something about Carter drew me like a magnet. When he'd dared me to tell him to stop that day, I hadn't wanted to.

I never wanted him to stop.

But things were so much more complicated now. And not just because of Liam. Because Carter was my boss. Because we worked together, and no matter how hard I tried not to, I liked him. I *really* liked him.

I wasn't sure when or how, but I knew that this little fantasy world we were in was going to collapse one day. Then I'd be alone again. If I allowed myself to fall for him, I was going to be left behind again in one way or another. And this time, the pain might be too much to bear.

This time, it was so much more than just a one-night stand with a man who *felt* different than the rest of them.

This time, my heart could be involved.

It just wasn't that easy not to fall for him. Yeah, sure, Carter was an asshole around the office. I'd realized that his employees didn't revere him as much as they feared him. He didn't treat them like shit, per se. But he was hard on them. He expected only the best—and he wanted more than they could possibly give. But with me, he was different. Kind and gentle. He treated me like a gentleman, although he still expected excellence from me. But he seemed to think highly of me.

He seemed to think I could give him what he needed, that I could give him the type of work I hadn't thought I could do at all.

I was involved in so much more than the design on this campaign. I was involved in marketing, and I dealt with the other team members a lot. I wasn't in charge of them, but sometimes it seemed like Carter expected me to be.

"You have to tell me everything," June said.

We sat at our favorite coffee shop. June and I were both taking our lunch hour. She worked for a large firm in town as the communications director—since college she'd worked her way up in the company and she was doing well for herself. She'd been away on business for the past two weeks, and I hadn't talked much to her about what was going on with Carter. It just wasn't the type of thing I wanted to talk about on the phone.

"What's there to tell?" I asked.

"Come on, you can't keep holding out on me. Tell me what it's like working with him at the office! You can't tell me it's just run-of-the-mill. I mean, he's the *father of your child.* God, if you clam up on me because I've been away on business, I'm never traveling again."

I laughed and shook my head. "It's just... weird to talk about. You know? I mean, it's Carter. *The* Carter. The man that's almost become a figment of my imagination."

"I know," June said with a sparkle in her eye. "And now he's real. And he's the father of your child."

"Will you stop saying that? I *know* that. I mean, I think about it all the time. But he doesn't know that, so it's easy enough to pretend he's just another person..." I groaned. "Who am I kidding. He's not just another person, not by a long shot. And we're getting closer."

"I knew it," June said with a smug smile. "If you're working together, it has to go one way or another. And it doesn't sound like it's going wrong. Is there chemistry between the two of you?"

I glanced up at her, blushing. "Yeah. I mean... yeah. A lot." I blushed harder, thinking about how he'd bent me over and fucked me on his desk.

June blinked at me. "Oh, my God. You slept with him?"

"How the hell do you know that?" I asked, giggling.

"It's written all over your face!"

I shook my head. "It was a mistake. We weren't supposed to do that. We're both professionals, and we work together. He's my boss. It was a mistake."

"You don't believe that for one second," June said with a wicked smile. "Was it amazing?"

I blushed again. "It was… but everything about him is amazing. I just…" My smile started fading, and I felt the worry that had been growing over the past two weeks creeping in. "We're really good together. And that's a problem."

"Why?" June asked.

A waiter brought the coffee we'd ordered and I grabbed my cup, taking a sip, holding onto the kick of caffeine as if it was a lifeline. June sipped hers, too, and glanced at the menu to remember what she'd decided on.

She ordered a Cobb salad. I ordered a gourmet sandwich.

When the waitress disappeared, June turned her attention back to me, waiting for an answer.

"Because I'm in danger of falling for him. And I haven't told him about Liam."

"So, tell him."

I shook my head and sipped my coffee. "It's not that easy."

"I know it's not," June said gently. "But he's here now, and you're hitting it off so well. If you tell him, you could be more. You could be—"

"Together?" I interrupted her. "I don't know. My coworker said he was a major playboy. I don't want to get attached to someone who can't be a one-woman man. Or someone who can't commit like Ryan. If I do, and Carter breaks my heart, where will that leave me?"

June nodded, not having an answer.

"Besides, I have no idea how he's going to take the news, and that scares me. What if he freaks out about it? What if he never wants to see me again? Or worse, what if I lose my job?"

"He won't fire you," June stated.

"Why not?"

"Because that would be wrong. Unethical. You have HR on your side with that."

I nodded. "I guess so. But still…"

I had no idea how I was going to approach it. When I'd seen him first, I'd been sure it was a sign. That he was back in my life had to mean that he deserved to know, and that this family didn't have to be broken anymore. I had fantasized countless times about what it might be like to have him in our lives, to have him help me with the costs, to spend time with him and Liam together. To be a family.

But I couldn't tell him. Maybe it would be better to keep quiet and just suffer through all of this. Maybe it was better if I didn't tell him at all.

"I don't know what to do," I finally said.

"I think you should follow your gut," June offered. "You've always done the right thing no matter how hard it was. You kept Liam and you raised him, and that's not an easy task. You'll figure this out, too."

I nodded. Our food arrived and we started talking about other things. It was easier to make small talk than to talk about the big things that were so hard to face.

After lunch, Carter was waiting for me in my office when I arrived.

"Oh," I said when I saw him. "Did I forget about a meeting or something?" I feverishly ran through my calendar in my mind.

"No," Carter said and grinned at me. His eyes were the color of a clear autumn sky and his smile made me feel weak at the knees. "I just wanted to see you."

I shook my head. "You can't do this, you know."

"What?"

"Come into my office to flirt with me."

He chuckled. "I'm the boss. I can do whatever I want."

"So, you flirt with your employees?"

I sat down behind my desk so that he had to turn to face me.

"Employee," he said. "Singular. You."

I nodded and looked at my computer, trying not to drown in those eyes.

"We should go out sometime," he said.

I looked up at him, surprised. "Go out?"

"Yeah. Like a date."

"I don't think that's a good idea," I said immediately. Even though I believed it was the best idea. Even though I wanted to go out with him so badly. And then go home with him. And then let him have his way with me.

But Liam popped into my mind, and my throat closed up. I was too scared to tell Carter about the son we had together. I was too scared that this—whatever it was—would fall apart the moment he knew.

I wanted to hold onto what we had as long as I could.

And at the same time I knew that wherever this was going, it wasn't going to work. It couldn't. Not in the long term.

"Why not?" he asked.

"Because we work together," I said.

Carter chuckled and walked around my desk. My breath caught in my throat when he swiveled my chair to face him, his hands leaning on the armrests so that his face was only inches away from mine.

"You can't use that as an excuse, Izzy." His breath was hot on my lips and I could see flecks of gray in his bright eyes. It was mesmerizing. Everything about him was intoxicating. I got drunk off the very idea of being with him.

When I didn't answer him, he brushed his lips against mine. The contact was so brief, I could have imagined it. He straightened up, a mischievous glint in his eyes.

"I'll get back to you for an answer a little later. I'll give you some time to think about it."

He sauntered out of my office, and I watched him go.

God, he was driving me crazy. I wasn't supposed to get this close to him. I wasn't supposed to allow this to happen. The idea had been to push him away.

But I couldn't think straight when I was around him. I couldn't focus on anything other than the taste of his lips and the feel of his hands on my skin.

How was I supposed to resist him?

I scrubbed my face with my hands.

God, I was in trouble. *Deep* trouble.

Carter was everything he'd been that night five years ago. And more. He was everything I wanted in my life. And at the same time, I knew that this was asking for pain and hurt. This was going to end in disaster. Men like him just didn't happen to women like me.

It had taken me five years to learn that no matter how hard I worked, life could still plant me on my ass whenever it felt like it.

A fairy tale life with Carter was a beautiful dream. But a fantasy like that brought hope, and hope was a dangerous thing when I knew a future with him might be a long shot.

No matter how good things felt right now.

I had to protect myself and Liam.

But when Carter looked at me like that, when he made advances that were impossible to resist, it was harder than anything to do the right thing.

CHAPTER 14

CARTER

*S*he was playing hard to get, damn her. And it was only turning me on more.

Every woman I'd come across had thrown herself at me the moment she found out who I was and what I was worth. I was used to women wanting to jump my bones the moment they met me.

There was no doubt that Isabelle wanted me just as badly as the rest of them, but she was different than them. She seemed to respect me for who I was as a person, and didn't seem to give a shit about my status and how much money I had.

It was refreshing. And it caused me to start looking at who I really was as a person. What was I showing her? What face did I wear for the world to see? For so long, I'd been strangely isolated, stuck in a world that didn't care about who I was because it cared about what I had. But Izzy cared about who I was.

She cared about the person under the suit.

And fuck, it made me want her. It made me want her so damn much, I could barely contain myself. I ached for her.

And unlike every other woman I'd sent away after I'd had my way, I wanted to see Izzy again. I wanted to fuck her again and again. In every position, in every location, in every *way possible. That* was new. That was weird.

I couldn't stop thinking about the day I'd fucked her on my desk. Screw office fantasies, that had been the ultimate. Not because of how hot it was and how cliché it was that I, the CEO, fucked one of my employees on my desk. But because it was Izzy. And she was like fire in my veins. She was everything I'd never found in another woman. Not in the five years I'd been searching.

And for some reason, she thought *this*—whatever was happening between us—was a bad idea.

What the fuck was bad about it? The only thing I could see, hear, *feel* when I looked at her, was good.

Very fucking good.

I wanted more. I wanted all of it.

Damn it, my cock was hard in my pants again. It happened all the time lately. In the weirdest places. Like at the office, when I was usually bored stiff. Ha. And in meetings where she was present.

Especially in meetings where she was present.

And I was headed into another one just like that.

The conference room was filled with the entire design team, including Austin and Derek Grimes, who hadn't gotten over the fact that I'd poached Izzy to work directly for me. When I stepped in, the room fell quiet and Grimes glowered at me from the corner where he'd holed up.

"Thank you for getting together on such short notice," I said. See? I could be nice to them even though they had no choice but to do as I asked when I asked. I glanced at Izzy before I continued. "The launch is getting closer and closer and excitement is in the air. So far, I'm seeing good work and I want to see more of it."

They all looked surprised. So, maybe I didn't usually thank them or commend them for doing good work. Maybe Izzy inspired me to be a nicer person. Someone she could see herself with, one day. Maybe I wasn't just an asshole all the time.

Well, okay, I was. But I was trying.

I launched into another set of bullet points of things I needed done as soon as possible, and when I started snapping commands, my staff looked a little more at ease. The fact that they were uncomfortable with me being nice was something I probably needed to take note of.

But my mind wasn't on them or the work we discussed. It was on Izzy the whole time. She took notes, looking composed and professional.

I flashed on images of her naked, spread across my desk. I flashed on the sound of her moaning when I licked and sucked on her pussy.

And my cock twitched in my pants.

"I think that's all for today," I said, adjourning the meeting. I couldn't think straight anymore.

Hell, whenever she was around me, I couldn't think straight at all.

When the team dispersed, leaving the conference room one by one, I cleared my throat.

"Miss Taylor," I said, addressing her in front of the others. "Please stay behind a moment."

She glanced at me and swallowed. Felicity raised her eyebrows before she squeezed Izzy's arm in support.

When everyone was gone, Izzy turned to me.

"What can I do for you?" she asked politely.

"You know what you can do for me," I said, taking a step closer.

Her eyes darkened when she looked up at me. Her lips were parted and plump and so fucking kissable.

"I don't think so," she said, and I wasn't sure if she meant she didn't know, or she didn't want to go out with me.

I closed the last bit of distance between us, and her breath caught in her throat. God, I loved it when she got flustered around me like that.

"Come out with me," I said.

She swallowed hard and shook her head no, but it wasn't very convincing. I stared into her eyes and her gaze slid to my lips. It was only a moment. But it was there.

Bingo.

I pulled her in closer for a kiss.

She hesitated for just a moment before she kissed me back. Her arms snaked around my neck and I pulled her body tightly against mine. Thank God I'd arranged the meeting with the design team in one of the conference rooms with solid walls rather than glass partitions. Because there was no way in hell I was going to stop myself from getting whatever Izzy was willing to give me, and if the rest of the company saw it, we were going to be in a world of trouble.

I could just imagine Hannah from HR getting her panties in a twist about the whole damn thing.

I stopped thinking about Hannah and rules and the rest of the company and focused on Izzy. My tongue was in her mouth, my body pressed against the length of hers, and I ground my hips against her so she could feel just how hard I was for her. I wanted her so fucking badly, I was already entertaining thoughts of stripping her naked and fucking her on the conference room table. The door had a lock, right? I couldn't remember.

But we could figure it out. Hell, I could even fuck her up against the door to prevent any chance of anyone trying to get into the room.

The idea made me hotter. Izzy's soft moans and whimpers into my mouth as we kissed and groped each other just fired me up that much more.

Suddenly, she pulled back, breaking the kiss. She breathed hard, her breasts heaving and falling.

"We shouldn't do this," she said, swallowing hard and running her hands through her hair, trying to compose herself.

"Why not?" I asked. "Don't you want this?"

"God, I want it so bad," she breathed. "But this..." She took a deep breath and let it out in a shudder. She looked at me and her eyes were filled with hunger and need. But under it all, there was sense. Izzy was responsible.

Fuck, I loved that about her.

And I hated it.

"I should focus on work," she said. "I need to get back to my office, and we shouldn't... *distract* ourselves."

I blinked at her. She was choosing work over me? How was that possible?

Women never told me 'no.' They never turned me down. The fact that Izzy was doing it was hard to understand—no, *impossible* to understand.

And for some reason, that only made me hotter for her.

Women always threw themselves at me, and as flattering as that was, it got old. This was new. Izzy was a breath of fresh air. And the fact that she respected herself, and chose something important over what she wanted, made me respect her.

"Fine," I finally said. "Focus on your work. But you can't leave me like this with nothing to hold onto."

A smile played over her lips. "What?"

"You have to give me something. Some sign, some... I don't know. Say you'll go out with me."

"What do you need a sign for?" she asked. Her eyes were almost laughing at me now.

I shrugged, feeling like a schoolboy who didn't know how to talk to a girl. Who was asking for attention and not just demanding it. The sensation was new.

"Say you'll go out with me," I said.

She hesitated, but a smile spread across her face. "Sure," she said. "I'll go out with you sometime."

She walked to the conference room door.

"Sometime?" I asked.

She looked over her shoulder, the look so fucking coy I wanted to yank her back and kiss her. Touch her. Taste her. Fuck her.

"Yeah," she said. "Isn't that enough to hold onto?"

She disappeared, and I stood in the middle of the conference room with a raging erection in my pants and confusion swirling in my mind.

God, this woman was driving me crazy. I was in deep shit. Because I liked her. I *really* liked her. And no matter what she did, I couldn't stop myself from falling more and more. She was pushing me away. She was rejecting me. She was playing hard to get. And that just made it worse.

At least she'd said she was going to go out with me. *Sometime.* It was better than nothing. I took a breath and willed the damned erection to go away. Luckily, it did just in time.

Austin appeared in the door.

"What the fuck are you doing?" he asked.

"Thinking," I said.

Austin barked a laugh. "That's new."

I rolled my eyes at him and laughed. "Screw you, man. What do you want?"

"We have to discuss shit, remember? You asked me to be in your office after the meeting. So I was there, waiting for you. Are you coming, or what?"

"Sure," I said. "Do I need to remind you that you work for me? If I want to make you wait, I can."

"You're an asshole," Austin laughed.

We walked together to my office, ready to get down to business. Austin was my best friend and we'd been in business together for years. It had always worked out.

I considered telling him about Izzy, about how things were progressing between us.

"So, when are you going back?" Austin asked as soon as we were in my office.

"What?"

"New York. When are you going back there?" he asked again.

Fuck. Somehow, I'd forgotten completely about New York. I'd forgotten all about leaving this world behind and going back to the place that had been my home for the past few years.

Or maybe I'd just been trying not to think about it.

"I don't know," I admitted.

"No? You're usually so eager to leave."

I shrugged. "I guess I'm enjoying being involved in the launch process."

"Are you okay?" Austin asked.

I laughed. "Why do you ask?"

"Because you never enjoy being involved in the process. Not like this. You just do the finance and the food. That's what you always tell me."

I shrugged again. "I guess I'm trying something different."

Austin narrowed his eyes at me. "Or you're doing *someone* different."

"What the fuck is that supposed to mean?"

Austin shrugged his shoulders. "I don't know. You usually follow your dick around more than your head. So, if you're staying here, you're getting some good pussy."

I shook my head. "What if I'm just interested in the company I started?"

"Sure," Austin said. "Let's pretend it's that until you decide to tell me what's really going on."

I forced a laugh and insisted that we start looking at work. I hated how well Austin could read me sometimes.

The thing was, Izzy wasn't just 'some good pussy.' She was everything.

And if I left, I would have to leave her behind.

I hadn't thought about that. I hadn't thought about anything other than her, and getting closer and closer to her.

But now that Austin had mentioned New York, unease swirled in the pit of my stomach.

What if I didn't want to leave her behind?

CHAPTER 15

ISABELLE

*I*t was the end of the month. I had worked at Appetite for just about three weeks now, and I was at the very end of my financial line. I'd stopped doing freelance jobs, and I didn't work at the restaurant anymore. My job at Carter's business was more than full-time.

I sometimes stayed late. I put everything I had into my new job to prove that I deserved it, to be sure that I kept it, and to show that I was a good investment.

But money was starting to dry up. I would get my first official paycheck soon. I just had to make sure I made it another few days, and then we would be golden.

Then everything would be okay again.

My life had already changed drastically since I'd started working at Appetite. My hours were stable, and Liam and I spent more time together than I'd ever had with him. I loved being able to see him, to chat with him, to just spend time together. I'd missed so many of his milestones because I'd been working myself to death so that we could survive.

Now that we were spending more time together, every-thing had changed. I was less stressed with a stable job, and

Liam seemed more content. I was more present with him, and we were closer than we'd ever been.

My mom didn't keep him for me anymore except to give me the odd night off so I could go for a drink or two with Bernie and June. I had him enrolled in a preschool program so he would be cared for until I picked him up after work, and he loved it.

"Come on, come on," I muttered, struggling to put together the last things for the big project deadline. I'd been killing myself over this the past couple of days, but I just couldn't get it right. I was a designer, an artist, for crying out loud.

And for some reason, Carter had pushed me more toward the marketing side. I had no idea what I was doing.

I reached for my phone to call down to Felicity to help me. She often jumped in and guided me in the right direction and I was so grateful to have someone like her to help me when I got stuck.

Lately, it felt like I got stuck all the time.

Before I could call Felicity, though, my cell phone rang. Liam's preschool number popped up on the screen, and my stomach twisted. I always panicked when they called—what if something terrible had happened? He was the most precious thing I'd ever had in my life. Sometimes, the thought of losing him, of something happening, woke me up in a cold sweat in the middle of the night.

"Isabelle, it's Monica," his teacher said over the phone. "I think you should pick Liam up. It's nothing too serious, but he's burning up and he keeps complaining he feels sick."

I glanced at my project. God, this was the worst time to leave. I needed to get this done. But Liam needed me. And he came first, no matter what.

"I'll be right there," I said.

I could always work on the project at home and send it in

tonight. As long as it reached Austin by midnight, I would be okay, right? It wouldn't matter where I was when I worked on it.

I packed up my things and hurried out of the office, hoping to God no one saw me leave. Leaving early was frowned upon by HR, and I didn't want to explain what my emergency was.

I rode the elevator to the lobby, and managed to escape the building without anyone stopping me and asking me where I was going.

When I got in the car, I rushed to Liam's preschool as fast as I could. I hoped it was nothing serious—as soon as I got paid, I would be able to afford medication and doctor visits, but right now, I had nothing to pull us through.

I parked a short distance away from the preschool and got out, hurrying down the road. When I arrived at the preschool, Monica sat with Liam on the front step, waiting for me. He looked wilted, his eyes drooping, his dark hair matted to his skin where he was sweating.

"Oh, honey," I said, pulling him into a hug. "I'm sorry you're sick."

"My tummy hurts," he said and wrapped his arms around his torso.

"I know, baby. We're going to take you home." I turned to Monica. "Thank you for calling me."

"I hope it's nothing too serious. We have a bug going around, a twenty-four-hour thing. But better get it checked out to be sure."

I nodded. "Thank you," I said.

We crossed the road and walked to my car. Liam walked slowly, hunched over a little, and I was worried something was seriously wrong. He looked like he was in pain.

"Honey, where does it hurt?" I asked, kneeling.

"Everywhere," he complained. "Even in my head."

I nodded my head in sympathy. Kids weren't always very good at explaining where the pain came from or what they felt.

My phone rang. I fumbled for it and saw Carter's caller ID on the screen.

"Shit," I said.

"You're not supposed to say that," Liam scolded meekly.

"I know," I said and pressed the phone against my ear.

"How is the project coming along?" Carter asked.

I was relieved he wasn't saying anything inappropriate.

"It's coming along okay," I said, wondering if I should be honest about it. Maybe if I was, he could allocate what was left to someone like Felicity, who knew what she was doing. "I'm struggling a little with the marketing plan that you sent last week. This isn't my forte."

"Yeah, I know. That's why I'm calling. I want to make sure you're on top of it."

"I'm not," I said. "I think it would be better if someone else finishes up. I'm going to make a mess of things, I just know it."

Please, give it away, take the bait, I willed. If I could hand this off to someone else, it would take off the pressure and I could take care of Liam.

"Nonsense," Carter said, and I groaned inwardly. "This is how you learn. By doing it. I'll come to your office and we'll go through it together."

"No," I said and squeezed my eyes shut.

"Why not?"

I hesitated, but there was no way I was getting out of this one.

"Because I'm not in the office." I steeled myself for the response.

"Where the hell are you?" Carter asked. But he continued

before I could answer. "I'll meet you. We'll go through it in person. Experience is the best teacher."

He wanted to meet with me in person? Now? I panicked.

"I'll figure it out," I said.

Liam groaned and clutched his arms around his stomach again.

"Yeah, sure. With my help," Carter said. "Where are you? I'll meet you."

I wasn't going to get out of this. And I needed Carter to see that I was serious about this job. I needed him to pay me. I needed to keep working at Appetite so that Liam could have the life he deserved.

With my mind confused and panicking, I couldn't think straight. Before I could come up with anything better, I gave Carter the nearby intersection.

"I'll be right there," he said and ended the call before I could say anything.

"Are we going home?" Liam asked.

I nodded. "Soon, baby. We just need to do something for Mommy's work."

"Your new work?"

"Yeah, so I can keep working there and we can keep spending time together."

"Okay," Liam said.

A short while later, a black car pulled up to the curb, and Carter stepped out of the back seat. He closed the door behind him, and the car left again.

He has a driver? I mused silently.

"You came here right away?" I asked.

Carter nodded and smiled, but his eyes trailed to Liam and his smile gave way to a frown.

"And who are you, little man?" he asked.

Liam looked up at Carter and the resemblance between the two made my heart constrict.

"Liam," my little boy said with confidence. "Who are you?"

Carter glanced at me before answering Liam. "I'm Carter."

"My tummy hurts so bad," Liam said. "I should never have eaten all of Olivia's candy."

"You ate too much candy?" I asked. "How much did you eat?"

Liam looked guilty, but then he took on a strange green color.

"Uh-oh, Mommy," he said and doubled over. He heaved and wretched and promptly threw up.

Right on Carter's shoes.

Fuck.

CHAPTER 16

CARTER

*W*hat the fuck was going on here? Why the hell did Izzy have a little munchkin with her? And what the fuck was he doing throwing up all over my shoes?

What the hell was happening?

Izzy scrambled into action as soon as the kid puked on me, grabbing a wad of tissues from her handbag. She kneeled in front of me, trying to wipe the vomit from my new Italian loafers.

"Don't bother," I said irritably. "They're ruined now. These aren't the type of shoes you just wipe clean like that."

"I'm so sorry," she said.

"I'm sorry," the kid echoed.

Who the hell was this kid? Why was Izzy here during working hours with a kid? None of it made sense.

Was she an au pair? Was this a nephew or a niece? Was this some kind of charity project?

I tried to answer my own questions but none of them made sense and it was almost comical to see her squirming to fix my shoes, which wouldn't make a difference.

"Izzy, get up," I ordered.

She sat back on her heels and glanced up at me.

Fuck, I liked her on her knees in front of me.

But any sexual fantasies soon evaporated with the little kid staring up at me with big brown eyes.

He looked eerily familiar now that I got a good look at him. Who was he? Where had I seen him before? I had a feeling I knew him, but... at the same time I knew he was a stranger.

Liam, he'd said his name was.

Slowly, Izzy climbed to her feet and looked at me with reddening cheeks.

"It's just been a tough day," she said.

"I can see that," I said dryly. "Do you want to explain to me why you're not in the office?"

"Liam is sick," she said.

"Yeah, I saw that, too," I said and glanced at my shoes. I wriggled my toes in the leather shoes, grateful that my socks weren't soaked in puke, too.

Izzy blushed deeper. She was mortified.

Liam's face was open, and he stared at me as if I was someone to gawk at. He wasn't too embarrassed about the fact that he'd just emptied his guts onto my shoes. Kids were so weird. They didn't seem to worry about social etiquette at all.

"I need to take him to someone who can take care of him," Izzy finally mumbled. "If you let me take care of that, we can meet up for work."

"Who is he?" I asked.

"I'm Liam," he said again.

She smiled at me. "He's Liam." She looked down at him and held out her hand. He took it as if this was a normal routine. "Come on, let's get going."

She walked to the car and he followed, and I watched the pair, trying to figure out how they had answered all my questions and I still knew nothing at all.

I watched her as she strapped the boy into a car-seat with great care. She flashed me an apologetic smile when she was done, and climbed in behind the wheel. She turned the key in the ignition and the car whined and coughed... and didn't start.

She tried again, and the same whining sound filled the air. I could see her muttering through the window. In the back seat, Liam had his eyes closed and he looked pale and miserable.

Izzy tried a third time before she slapped her hand against the wheel and hung her head in frustration.

I straightened my tie and walked to the car. Someone needed to do something.

And it so happened that I had experience being a knight in shining armor.

I walked around the car and opened her door.

"It won't start," she said in a soft voice.

She looked like she was on the edge. Like she was very close to something cracking, to this being the last straw.

"I was supposed to get it serviced. I just... I thought I could wait until the end of the month when I got my first paycheck. I have to..."

"It's okay," I said.

My heart went out to her. She hadn't had it easy the past while, that was plain to see. The way her mouth was down-turned and the fact that she accepted difficulties with resignation were signs of someone who'd been through it a few times, who expected things to go wrong just because they didn't ever go right.

It shouldn't have been like this. The Isabelle I'd met five years ago had been full of life and light, and she'd had a spark about her that had ignited something warm inside of me, too.

This Isabelle was a little different. She was still Isabelle, and her light hadn't gone out completely, but it had dimmed considerably.

That spark was still there, though. The part of her that had woken the part of me.

And damned if I was going to let shitty circumstances snuff that part of her out and kill off what made her so magical in the first place.

"I'll take you home," I said.

"It's really okay—" she started, but I wasn't having any of it.

"Isabelle."

She blinked at me when I used her full name—I'd mostly been referring to her as Izzy whenever I saw her. She could hear the seriousness in my voice. Good.

"Okay," she finally said.

I picked up my phone and called my driver, who'd dropped me off here not too long ago. I'd figured I would go with Izzy to wherever we were going to work together.

The driver appeared in no time at all.

"Do you always have a driver on call?" Izzy asked.

I nodded. "In case I need to go somewhere."

"Convenient," she mumbled.

I took out my phone.

"What are you doing?" she asked.

"I'm calling roadside assistance to pick up your car and take it in."

"Oh, no, please don't," she said, shaking her head. "I can't afford to get it fixed right now. I'll call someone and we can tow it back to my place until—"

I put my hand on her arm and she stopped talking.

"I'm having them take it to the shop and they'll fix it. We'll figure the rest out later, okay?"

She wanted to argue, but what was she going to say? I was adamant, and she needed a working car.

"Get the kid, and get in the car." My commands were snappy when I didn't need them to be. But I was covered in puke, and seeing Izzy with a kid she needed to look after made me feel uncomfortable. I didn't know why I felt that way, and that made me even more irritated.

She unbuckled the kid, removed his car-seat, and helped him out of the car. I eyed him suspiciously. He looked pale and sweaty, as if he was working up a fever. He was clearly sick. Was he going to puke again? If he barfed all over my leather seats, I was going to be annoyed.

Not at either of them, because that would make me a dick. But I had everything in my life just the way I liked it. The puke on my Italian loafers was already a setback I tried not to be too irritated about.

She loaded the kid's car-seat into the back seat, then helped the boy climb into the contraption. She sat next to him. I slid in with them, too, with Isabelle in the middle.

Izzy pressed her hand against the kid's head.

"Does he have a fever?" I asked.

"He doesn't," she said, and she looked relieved. "But I'll still give him something when you drop us off."

I nodded and turned my head toward the window. The rest of the journey was made in silence. I didn't know what to say, Izzy looked worried, and the boy was too sick to be talkative, from the looks of it.

When we arrived at the address Izzy had given the driver, I looked up at a tall building of apartments all squashed in together. We climbed three flights of stairs—Izzy carried Liam up the last flight—and she unlocked one of the three paint-flaked doors on the landing where we stood.

"I'm sorry for the mess," she said over Liam's shoulder. "I didn't expect guests and I haven't had time to straighten up."

"Don't worry about it," I said.

She nodded and pushed the door open. I followed her into the apartment.

"I'll be right back," she said and disappeared down a short hallway.

I stood in the apartment and looked around.

The place wasn't great. It was small and cramped. Her living room furniture barely fit, the couches were far too close to the television, and the open-plan kitchen had a large brown water mark against the ceiling where I was guessing there had been a leak not too long ago. Or there still was.

This was all wrong. When I'd met Izzy, she'd been a breath of fresh air, a dash of color in a life that had otherwise gone stale and gray for me. I'd imagined her in front of a canvas in a grand art studio, wearing coveralls, with music blaring in the background and paint splatters on her face and hands. I'd expected a life for her that was carefree and golden.

Not this. I'd imagined a lot of things in the time I'd been thinking about her, but none of my thoughts had come close to this.

She wasn't supposed to live in this condition, in a dark, rundown apartment.

She deserved better than this.

I was going to help her. I was going to give her more than this. But something told me she wouldn't accept my help without a fight. She was stubborn like that.

I looked at a framed picture of the kid on her wall. Liam. I hadn't gotten a good look at him before, since he'd been in the throes of illness, and the whole thing had been kind of a blur.

But if the fact that they lived together hadn't given it away, I could tell from the family resemblance in the photo that he was her son. He had her eyes, her hair, and her mouth. Cute kid.

But there was something more there. Something in his face.

It felt familiar. It reminded me of my childhood photographs from my dad's house.

My stomach tightened and my heart sped up.

Was Liam *my* son, too?

CHAPTER 17

*L*iam still didn't have a fever, thank God. I took his temperature, then I helped him get out of his school clothes and into pajamas. I checked again when he climbed into bed, just to be sure. I tucked him in and pulled the cover right up to his chin, and I planted kisses on his face until he offered a weak giggle.

That was all I needed. I needed him to look more like himself.

I felt like everything was going wrong right now, and it was getting to me. Work was a challenge—it had been since day one. I was grateful for my job, but some afternoons I came home with a head that felt like an old sponge. I just needed this month to end so I could get paid and work could ease up again.

"How do you feel, sweetheart?" I asked Liam. "Is your tummy still sore?"

He shook his head. "It's a little better."

"I'm glad," I said. "I think you need to nap a little bit, and when you wake up, you'll feel a lot better."

He nodded and yawned sleepily, not even fighting me on

having to take a nap. Usually, it was a war just to get him into bed.

He fell asleep almost right away. When I was sure he was going to be okay, I left his room and quietly pulled the door shut behind me.

I took a deep breath to collect myself, put on a bright face, and walked back to the living room where I'd left Carter. He stood in the middle of the room, looking around. I cringed a little—he was seeing parts of me that weren't all that pretty.

I hadn't wanted him to see the personal side of my life. He liked me so damn much, and a part of me had figured that if I could keep him at arm's length, keep whatever was going on between us at the office, he would never see anything that would change his mind about how much he liked me.

But he was seeing it all now. He was getting a glimpse behind the scenes, and it was a mess.

"How is he?" Carter asked when he saw me.

"I think it might just be a little bug. I'm hoping it is. He's not running a fever, and his teacher said there's a twenty-four-hour thing doing the rounds."

Carter nodded as if he understood. I didn't get the feeling he did.

I swallowed hard. My chest felt tight, the familiar panic setting in that I wasn't doing enough to take care of Liam. I didn't always know how to protect him, not when so much was out of my control.

"I'm sorry about all of this," I said.

"It's okay," Carter said.

"Can I offer you something to drink?" I asked.

Carter shook his head and pushed his hands into his pants pockets.

"So, Liam is your son, huh?" he asked.

I blushed, my cheeks going bright red. I wasn't ready for

this conversation just yet. I mean, I was planning to tell him soon. I'd just wanted it to be on my own terms.

But there was no denying it. It was time Carter knew the truth. I had to tell him. I couldn't hide it from him anymore, not after this. I took a deep breath, bracing myself.

"Yes," I finally said. "Liam's my son. And he's yours, too."

Carter didn't look shocked or surprised. He nodded slowly.

"Yeah, I thought so."

A part of me constricted. I wasn't sure what to expect. He didn't look angry with me. He looked… I wasn't certain *what* I was seeing on his face.

I sank onto the couch, dropping my head into my hands for a moment before I ran my fingers through my hair. I squared my shoulders and sat up. These were facts. I could apologize for them, but this was my life. I hadn't done anything wrong. In fact, the last five years had been as hard as they were because I'd been breaking myself doing the *right* thing.

"Why didn't you tell me?" he asked.

"You left," I said simply. "I didn't even know your last name back then. How was I supposed to find you?"

"And after I came back? You've been working for me for weeks, Izzy." His voice was hard, his eyes cold. So, he was angry after all. "How could you not tell me?"

A million thoughts ran through my mind. Apologies, rebuttals, excuses. But as I thought about them all, I became angry.

I didn't have to apologize for anything, or make excuses.

"What was I supposed to do?" I asked. The anger could be heard in my voice and for a moment, Carter looked surprised.

"You could have told me," he said, the surprise gone again and his irritated edge returned.

"You're right, I could have," I said. "But I didn't. I had to decide what was right, Carter."

"And you didn't think it was right to tell me that we have a child together? This is a big thing, Izzy. It's not just—"

"I know what it is," I snapped, interrupting him. "Do you think I didn't want to tell you?" I was getting angrier and angrier, but I kept my voice down so I wouldn't wake Liam. "I wanted you to know. Hell, I could have used the help, too. I sacrificed everything that was important to me to raise him. This wasn't where I saw myself five years ago. But this is the turn life took, and I'm doing my best to make sure I do right by him. You can't come in here telling me that I was wrong for not talking to you right away. It's not the type of thing you just throw into casual conversation."

He nodded. "You're right, it's not. But we've had serious conversations, too. We've had moments where you could have told me."

"When?" I asked. "Before or after the staff meetings where you put me on the spot because you like seeing me squirm?"

He pursed his lips.

"Or after you fucked me on your desk, was that a good time to bring it up? Or when we discussed the deadlines on a job you gave me that I'm not qualified for in the first place?"

"Hey, I gave you a job that I knew you were going to manage. It's a better position than you would have had. More money."

"Yeah, and I'm working directly for you," I added.

He snapped his mouth shut.

"Did you think I didn't know that was what it was?" I asked. "Did you think I was stupid?"

Carter shook his head. "That's the last thing I thought you were."

I nodded. So, he understood that I was standing on my

124

own two feet, I wasn't just being pushed around and toyed with.

"You're getting defensive, Izzy," he said.

I crossed my arms over my chest. He was right. I knew I should have told him about Liam from the first day I saw him again.

"I wanted to tell you," I said. "I just didn't know how. This isn't easy, you know. It hasn't been since the day I found out I was pregnant and the father of my baby disappeared into thin air."

I was suddenly bitter about the fact that I'd done it all alone. Even though I had no right to be. Carter hadn't abandoned me, he simply hadn't known. And I was partially to blame for that. Sneaking out before he woke up had seemed simpler—no strings attached, sex for the sake of sex, get out and keep taking care of myself. That was what I'd thought at the time. If I'd known that a baby would come of it, I would have acted differently.

But hindsight has always been perfect, and I hadn't known.

Being upset about how my life had turned out in comparison to his wasn't right. And still, I couldn't help it. Not only did Carter have fewer responsibilities, and he could live his life with all the freedom he wanted, but he had so much money he didn't have to worry about food or medical bills or getting his car serviced.

And I was scraping the bottom of the barrel on a good day.

"You're angry," Carter said.

"No shit," I snapped. "You would be, too."

"I *am* angry, right now. I have a right to be," Carter pointed out.

I shook my head. This was too much to handle. I felt like I was spinning in circles. My mind was going a mile a minute and my emotions were trying to keep up with what had happened, with the fact that Carter knew now.

I was exhausted. I dropped my head into my hands and rubbed my temples.

"I think you should go," I finally said.

"What?" Carter asked. He sounded surprised again.

I supposed today was a day filled with surprises. He'd just found out he had a child. He had puke on his shoes, and the woman that'd been working for him wasn't perfect the way he thought she was.

My life was boring and filled with responsibility. I had to work myself to death just to make ends meet, and I was pretty sure the image Carter had had of me in his mind was nothing like this.

He was probably through with me, too. It was better if I was the one to push him away. It would hurt less if I decided it instead of him. If I said it instead of him.

"It's better this way," I said. "Thank you for your help getting us home. I'll... try to figure out the project and get that in before tonight."

"Don't worry about it," Carter said in a clipped voice. "You have your hands full. I'll get someone else to take care of it."

Fear grabbed a hold of me. What did that mean? Was he going to fire me?

"I'm not going to fire you," Carter said as if he could read my mind. Maybe it was written all over my face. "But Liam is sick and you need to take care of him. I'm not going to be a dick about it and make you do this."

I didn't know what to say. Before I could think of anything, Carter walked to the door.

"I'll see you in the office, Izzy," he said over his shoulder. "Good luck."

When he left, I stared at the door he'd disappeared

through, trying to figure out how the hell everything had suddenly buckled and caved in on me like this. Carter knew now. He *knew*. And not just that, he wanted to know why I hadn't told him. Which meant he would have wanted to know. It meant... God, I wasn't sure exactly what it meant.

But the cat was out of the bag now.

And I had more to worry about. Carter had said he wasn't going to fire me, which was a relief. But what about my future? At the company, and with him. And what about Liam? What was going to happen now?

I'd asked Carter to leave and he'd been shocked. The truth was, I'd been shocked about the words coming out of my mouth, too. But it wasn't that simple. If Carter was in the picture, he had paternal rights to Liam.

After doing it on my own for so long, I didn't want to share Liam. After all, how well did I really know Carter? We'd shared one night together years ago, and I'd worked with him for less than a month. And I wasn't certain I was entirely thrilled about what I'd seen in that time.

I swallowed a lump in my throat.

What if Carter decided he wanted my son? With Carter's wealth and connections, surely he'd have access to powerful attorneys.

What if he took full custody?

The thought was too terrible to even comprehend, so I pushed it away. I couldn't lose my baby. I had to keep him safe. Keep him close to me.

Carter knew he was Liam's dad, but the truth only made me feel worse. There was no relief at finally having done the right thing. A crack had appeared in the carefully constructed wall I'd built around my life.

What if it all blew up in my face?

CHAPTER 18

CARTER

I felt like someone had pulled a rug from under me. I was reeling.

A son? I had a son?

And I'd never known. All this time, Izzy had been raising the boy. I'd been going on with my life carefree and oblivious to the fact that I was a father.

But that wasn't my fault. I had never been told the news. I was an absentee dad, but it wasn't my choice. If she'd told me at any point—if she'd managed to find me—I would have been there. I would have been a dad to the kid if I'd known.

Guilt threatened to overcome me, but I pushed it away. How could I have known? Of course, she'd had no way to contact me, but she could have told me when she'd seen me again. She *should* have told me. But she didn't.

And that wasn't my fault, either.

But now, I knew. I knew that I had a son, and I knew that Izzy and Liam weren't living in the best conditions. And even though she'd told me to get out, to leave, I wasn't going to just leave it there.

She deserved better. And so did he.

I climbed into the car that was still waiting for me in the street and directed the driver to take me back to the office. I had work to take care of—Izzy's project had to be handed off, for one. And I had to make sure everyone else who was taking care of the deadline was doing their jobs. The launch was pending and it needed to be taken care of.

But my mind wasn't fully on work. There was no way I was going to be able to focus on the product launch after what I'd just found out. I was the boss, and I was going to delegate my work to everyone else qualified to do it.

I had other things I wanted to take care of.

When I got to the office, I summoned Felicity into my office and gave her Izzy's work to finish.

"Is she okay?" Felicity asked when I wouldn't tell her why she needed to take over Izzy's work.

"She's okay," I said. "She just has a few personal things to take care of."

"Okay," Felicity said, happy with my answer. "I'll make sure this is ready."

"Thank you," I said.

Felicity left my office and as soon as she did, I did a quick search online. I picked up my phone. As the line connected, I stared at my workspace and flashed on the day I'd had Izzy naked on my desk, gasping and trembling and begging for more.

Fuck, everything about her was intoxicating. I wanted her again. I wanted her hard and fast, and slow and sensual, and in every way I could have her.

But things just weren't that simple anymore, were they? I still wanted her body, but I also wanted more from her. And now that I knew we had a child together... everything was going to have to change.

When someone answered, I brought myself back to the present.

"You're the best realtor in town?" I asked.

"Well, I don't like to brag, but..."

I rolled my eyes. His name was Rex Curtis and his name had popped up first when I'd searched for upscale realtors.

"I need a condo. Three bedrooms, two bathrooms, and something for a kid to keep himself busy with."

"I do have a place that's just become available," Rex said. "A very nice one. Would you like to have a look?"

"Do you have any photos you can send me?" I asked.

Rex obliged while we were still on the call, and an email came through with photos of the place. It was much better than the apartment Izzy was living in now. Not only was it in a good neighborhood, and closer to work, but the rooms looked light and spacious. The gated complex had secure parking and large grassy areas complete with a pool and playground where Liam could have a bit of fun.

"I'll take it," I said to Rex.

"Without seeing it?" he asked, incredulous.

"Are you telling me the photos aren't accurate? That I might find something I won't like?"

"Oh, no, not at all."

I nodded, satisfied. "Then I'll take it. Set it up. When is it available for occupation?"

"Immediately," Rex said.

Perfect.

I ended the call feeling good about myself. I wasn't sure where Izzy and I were going to go in terms of our relationship. I wasn't sure what was going to happen next. I wanted to be a part of Liam's life, but there were a lot of things to straighten out first.

Whatever happened, Izzy would always have a good job here at Appetite. She would never have to worry about job security again. And she would always have a place to stay that she wouldn't have to worry about, either. I was going to buy the place so she didn't have to worry about rent and upkeep.

I would do right by her, no matter what happened between us.

Something still nagged at the back of my mind, though. It was all well and good to make these plans, to put the practical things in motion, but having a child wasn't just about getting the formalities out of the way. It was about so much more than that.

What if she didn't want me to be a part of Liam's life? I didn't exactly lead the life of a model parent. Until recently, I'd fucked around. I'd partied. I'd lived my life to the hilt. And I had a very serious, strict way of dealing with my employees. They feared me, and I was a dick to them sometimes for no good reason other than that I *could* be. Because I was the boss.

But that was going to change. If I had a son that looked up to me, if I was to be held accountable, then I was going to do what needed to be done. I was going to step up and be the man Liam deserved to have as a role model.

God, I'd only been a father for two hours and I was already panicking about what it meant. Sure, technically I'd been a father for much longer than that, but I'd only found out about it today.

I tried to do a bit of work, now that a home for Izzy had been acquired, but I couldn't focus. I'd expected it, but it was still frustrating. I'd thrown myself into work since day one.

After wasting another hour staring at my laptop screen without getting anything done, I picked up my phone again. This time, I called my dad.

I took a deep breath as the phone rang.

"Carter," my dad said when he answered the phone.

"Hi, Dad," I said.

It was always so damn awkward with him. My father and

I didn't have the best relationship. We spoke now and then, but since my mom passed away when I was fourteen, our relationship had deteriorated, fast. She'd been the glue between us, the reason I'd done anything in my life.

The degrees, the company, all of it.

My dad hadn't really been around much, and I preferred it that way. I didn't get along with him. I felt like he'd never really understood me.

But I couldn't think of anyone else to call right now. My dad was… well, he was a *dad*. Though he'd never been a great father, he at least had some experience in that department. And now, after everything I'd found out, I needed someone to guide me in the right direction.

I wouldn't usually turn to him, but nothing about this was run-of-the-mill.

"It's good to hear from you, son," Dad said.

"Yeah…"

We were silent for a moment. I never knew exactly what to say to him. It was one of the reasons we talked so seldom.

"What's on your mind?" Dad finally asked.

"Well… I just found out I'm a father."

My dad whistled through his teeth.

"Yeah," I said. "I know."

He didn't scold me for being irresponsible. My life was none of his business. At least he knew that much.

"I just…" I took a deep breath. "I don't know what to do."

"Do you want a part of it?" Dad asked. "More than the monetary support I'm assuming you're going to offer."

"Yeah," I said. "I do. I want to be a part of it. The mother of the kid is great, Dad. Not just, you know, a fling. Well, she was once upon a time, but it's different now. I guess we're still trying to figure that part out. But as for the child, I don't know if she wants me around."

"Have you talked to her about it?"

132

"No," I admitted. "Our conversation was strained and it ended abruptly."

"It's a big thing for her to tell you," Dad said. "And if you only found out now... how old is the kid?"

"Four, according to my calculations."

My dad whistled through his teeth again. I lowered my forehead to my desk and rested it there.

"She's been doing it alone all this time?" he asked.

I stilled. I didn't know the answer to that question. Had she been dating? Had she been married? God, just the thought of some other guy in the picture pissed me off. The idea that someone else could have been where I wanted to be...

"I don't know," I said. "Maybe."

"It's hard to take a step back when you've been doing it alone. When your mother passed..."

He didn't know how to finish his sentence, but I knew what he was trying to say. I had been young, and it had just been the two of us. I'd been at home for a few years before I left for college, and my dad had mostly taken care of me alone.

"She's going to have a tough time stepping back and making space if it's just been the two of them all this time," he said.

I nodded. He had to be right about that point. She'd become so defensive when I'd asked her why she didn't tell me. And she'd made sure I knew how much she'd sacrificed. Fuck, if I'd been there, she wouldn't have had to sacrifice anything.

It now made sense why she'd dropped out of college.

"What am I supposed to do?" I asked. "I have no idea what to do."

"I think you should tell her that you're willing to be there. And let everything go at her pace. One thing at a time. This isn't going to be a rush job. And if she doesn't want you to be a part of the picture at all, you can stand on your right to know your son. But no matter what, you should respect her."

My father was right. Wise. He was emotionally detached from the whole situation, so he could be objective. My thoughts were so mixed up, I could hardly think straight.

"And, son," my dad said. "It's going to be okay. You just do what you need to do, and trust that the rest will fall into place. Step up and be the man I raised you to be, and it's going to work itself out."

I wanted to ask him what would happen if it wasn't okay. But that wasn't something I could talk to him about. We weren't close enough for that. And there was only so much of my emotions I was willing to share with him.

"Thanks, Dad," I said instead. "I appreciate it."

"Anytime. I mean it, Carter."

We ended the call and I put my phone down on my desk, staring at it until the screen dimmed.

I had to step up and be a man. That I could do. I was going to take care of them as much as I could. But if Izzy didn't want me in her life... I would have to respect that.

I didn't want to believe that was even possible—that she didn't want me in her life. Not after everything we shared. Not with our insane chemistry, that spark between us...

But things weren't that simple anymore, were they?

The truth was out in the open. We had a son together. What if the connection we shared wasn't enough now that everything was suddenly so complicated?

CHAPTER 19

ISABELLE

*L*iam looked a lot better in the morning, and I was relieved.

Still, to be sure, my mom said that she would watch him instead of me taking him to preschool, and I could go back to work without worrying. I hadn't wanted to saddle her with the responsibility—she had done so much to help me out with him when I had juggled so many jobs—but she'd insisted she wanted to help. Now that he went to preschool and I was taking care of everything by myself, she didn't see him nearly as often as before. I knew she wanted to spend some time with him.

I was glad—it was one less thing to worry about. She would call me if anything went wrong, but when I dropped him off this morning, his eyes were bright, his temperature was good, and he didn't look so pale and miserable. He had been in a good mood.

My mind had already been spinning about work. Carter had made sure that Felicity would take over my project, and for that I was grateful. Not only because I had been taking care of a sick child, but because I hadn't been completely sure what I was doing in the first place. Now, at least, I knew that everything was okay with the deadline, and that Carter's launch would be a success.

But that wasn't the part that had me grinding my teeth with worry at night, and had me distracted this morning when I'd made us breakfast, barely picking up on Liam's happy chatter.

Carter knew about Liam. I had no idea what was going to happen now. I'd always been in control of everything, and even though it hadn't been easy, I'd always been the one in charge.

I'd struggled with money, I'd juggled jobs, I'd tried my best—and failed—to give him the life I wanted him to have. But I'd been the one to do it all. I'd been the one jumping through hoops and pulling strings and doing everything that could be done.

For the first time in a long time, I had no idea what was going to happen.

My stomach twisted in a knot of nerves and my palms were sweaty. How was I going to face him today? I had been the one to tell Carter—in so many words—that Liam was his, but he'd been the one to put all the missing pieces together and see the whole picture. I should have known that he would figure it out when he came to meet us. Liam was the spitting image of him.

I was pretty damn sure everything was going to change between us. How could it not? It had been nearly five years since he'd become a father, and Carter hadn't known anything. That wasn't my fault. At least, not at first. But Carter had been right to ask me why I hadn't told him right away.

I knew that I should have, it had been the right thing to do. I'd worried about it from the start. From the moment I'd seen Carter in that conference room, smirking at me.

It had been so easy to keep it a secret, easier than having to talk to him. And there had been the matter of protecting my little boy. It had been the two of us for so long, it was difficult to think that now I was going to have to let another person into the little world I'd created for us.

As soon as I arrived in my office, I found a note on my desk. Carter was asking me to meet with him.

My stomach twisted and turned and I felt sick with panic. Feverishly, I tried to think of a way to get out of this. But I didn't have any excuse—there were no pending meetings and my sudden onslaught of nausea was because I was scared, not because I'd picked up Liam's stomach bug. I was going to have to face the music at some point. It was better to get it over and done with as soon as possible.

As I walked to his office, my mind ran over every possibility. *Carter's furious that I didn't tell him. He wants Liam in his life. No, he wants to take him from me. He doesn't want to see me anymore. He could care for Liam in a way I never could, pay for the best education, the best home, the best everything. He's going to fire me.*

The further I walked, the worse the thoughts became.

Stop it, I scolded myself. I was just going to work myself into a frenzy for no reason. I couldn't react until I knew what was going to happen.

I knocked on Carter's door and swallowed a lump down my throat. "You wanted to see me?" I asked when he looked up.

Carter nodded and beckoned me in. "Take a seat, Izzy."

I did as he asked. The office seemed chilly and goosebumps broke out over my skin. Carter was all business, his face serious, his eyes on his laptop screen. He clicked away, working on something without saying another word.

We sat in silence for a moment.

Finally, he finished whatever he'd been doing and looked up.

It felt like he saw right through me, and I fought the urge to squirm. His eyes were icy and intense, as usual. I always had to stop myself from falling into them—I couldn't swoon over a man who might tell me that he wants nothing to do with me anymore.

"So, yesterday was a surprise…" Carter started.

I nodded, twisting my fingers together. "I'm sorry about that."

Carter shook his head. "It's okay. I think I understand."

Did he? But he was trying, and that was something.

"I understand if everything changes between us," I started, getting on with it. He wasn't getting to the point and I was getting more and more nervous. He was being *understanding*, and that made me uncertain. I'd expected a storm.

Carter frowned. "Why would anything change?"

I stared at him, my face clearly showing what I thought.

"Okay, okay," he said, nodding and holding up his hands. "Of course, everything is going to change. But I don't want anything to change between *us*."

I blinked at him, not knowing what to say.

"I know that nothing can be the same as before," he continued. "But don't look so nervous. I don't want things to change between us—not in a negative way. I know that everything is going to change because this is serious. Because we have a child together."

God, just hearing him say those words was surreal. He had been almost like a figment of my imagination for so long, having him sit in front of me in person and talk about Liam as *our* son felt like a dream.

"We have to discuss business, though," Carter added.

"What kind of business?" I asked carefully.

"I got you a new apartment. A condo, actually."

My mouth dropped. "What?"

"The sale is already in motion, and you'll be able to move in by the end of the week."

"A condo?" I asked, trying to make sense of what he was saying.

"Yeah," he said. "It's new. And it's better than where you're staying now."

I heard the words, but I struggled to compute. A new home? It had been one day since Carter had found out, and now we were already moving? I struggled to process it, struggled to deal with the shock that came with the announcement. My ears rang and I felt dizzy.

Carter kept quiet and waited for me to work through the news. At first, the idea of a new home sounded exciting, but the more I thought about it, the more I started wondering what exactly it meant.

New? Better?

I got irritated. Angry, even.

"I've been doing the best I can," I said defensively. "The home I've provided for Liam isn't a bad one."

"It's not," Carter agreed. "In fact, you've been doing an incredible job, all on your own. I can't tell you how impressed I am by that. It's a big deal, Izzy."

Again, my jaw dropped. I hadn't expected him to act like this—to step up. And I definitely hadn't expected him to compliment me on the job I'd been doing. For so long, I had been aware of how much I had to sacrifice and that I'd been doing it all alone. I wasn't particularly bitter, I just... tried not to think too much about everything I'd lost. But now, Carter was sitting across from me, showing me that possibly he *did* understand.

"I don't know what to say," I finally admitted.

"Then look at this while you find the words," Carter said and turned his laptop toward me. On it, a litany of photos were scattered across the screen, showing me images of the perfect condo, with spacious rooms, beautiful finishes, and a playground and pool on the grounds.

"Are you serious?" I asked, looking at Carter.

"I'm not the joking type," he said gravely. "This is where you're going by the end of the week. And this is just the first of many things I'm planning on doing for the two of you."

The first of many? Carter was knocking my feet out from under me. How was this possible? He was doing everything he was supposed to do, and more. And it hadn't even been twenty-four hours since he'd found out about Liam.

It was so much to take in, my head was spinning.

"So?" Carter asked when I didn't say anything. I just stared at his laptop again. "What do you think? Do you think it will work for Liam?"

I thought that it was the most incredible place I'd ever seen. It was definitely going to work for Liam—it was perfect. He would love the playground, and in the hot summer days, going for a swim sounded divine. Not just for him but for me, too.

It was a lot to take in. And it was a lot to accept from a man I hadn't even known would be positive about the whole thing half an hour ago.

I nodded. "It will work."

"So, you'll take it?" Carter asked.

"Okay."

When I looked up at Carter, a grin had spread across his features.

"Yeah?" he asked.

I nodded. I would agree to moving into the condo. It was perfect for Liam, and our crappy apartment had been bugging me for a long time. A part of me wanted to fight it, to tell Carter that I could manage. But I wasn't managing, not completely, was I? And Carter was doing exactly what was expected of him—he was taking care of us. I couldn't argue with him about that, and I couldn't fault him on it.

It felt too good to be true, but somehow, it *was* true.

I was going to let this happen, I was going to allow him to take care of us the way that I had wished for since the moment I'd found out I was pregnant.

"Yeah," I said in agreement. "I can't believe it, I'm struggling to wrap my mind around it. But yes, we'd love to move in."

"Perfect," Carter said, rubbing his hands together. "I'll arrange for a moving company to collect your personal belongings as soon as the sale is through."

I wanted to argue again, but stopped myself. He was doing this for us. I had to let him. Liam deserved this, if nothing else. But a part of me, a little part that I hadn't allowed to show in a long, long time, agreed that for a change, I could say that I deserved it, too.

We both stood. Carter walked around the desk and reached out to me, giving my hand a little squeeze. Electricity jolted into me the way it always did when he touched me, and I was relieved it still felt the same between us. I hoped he felt it, too.

"Thank you," I said to Carter.

"Any time, Izzy," he said, and his eyes were caring.

My head felt light. So much was changing, and so fast. Excitement rushed through me as I pictured Liam's face when he saw his new home.

But Carter was buying the condo. Maybe this was his way of taking control over my life and Liam's. Maybe this was just the beginning.

Part of me still couldn't trust that Carter was as good as he appeared to be. And something in my core tensed up as I thought about that.

I could almost feel a bit of control slip from my hands.

CHAPTER 20

CARTER

I wanted to see him again. I wanted to get to know my boy.

I wasn't sure it was all so simple to me. The moment I'd seen him, something inside me clicked. It'd taken a moment for me to figure out that that kid, the one who'd puked all over my shoes, was mine. But the moment I figured it out, a part of me felt like this was the way it should have been all along.

The kid with the dark hair like mine. And the big, soulful eyes like Izzy's.

Best of both worlds.

I wanted to know if his personality was a perfect mixture of the two of us, too. I wanted to know what he was like, if I could see more of myself in him.

But it wasn't just about that. It was about a lot more. It went so much deeper than just wanting to get to know him because he was my blood.

When I was little, my family had been pretty close. My mom, my dad, and me. But it had been because of my mom. She'd been the glue that kept our family together. When she passed away, it felt like a part of me had died, too. And then my dad and I had started drifting apart. Not as much at first —I still lived at home and he had to take care of me to a certain extent. But as I grew up, studying and creating a life for myself, and eventually moving to New York, my dad and I had grown distant.

I didn't feel like he knew who I was anymore. I didn't feel like he understood me or my dreams for the future. And it was hard talking to him without our conversations being ruled largely by awkward silences.

I hadn't known about Liam, so I hadn't been there for the first part of his life, but there was still time. A lot of it. I wanted to get to know him. I wanted a relationship with him. I wanted to be close to him in the way my own dad and I *weren't* anymore.

And I wanted to get around to it as soon as possible. At some point—I wasn't sure when yet—I'd have to return to my offices in New York. It was my home, where I had my own apartment, and where I ran the New York branch of Appetite.

The idea of leaving Izzy and Liam behind caught in my throat. I pushed the thought aside as I drove my car toward the new condo Izzy and Liam were settling into.

When I walked up the front door, my stomach twisted. I lifted my hand to knock, but paused, catching myself.

I was nervous.

What the fuck?

He was just a kid, right?

But he wasn't just a kid. He was *my* kid. And this wasn't just about spending time together. It was about letting him know that I was his dad.

It had taken me a few days to persuade Izzy to let me officially meet him. The whole week, I'd brought up the topic. She'd been reluctant at first, and I understood it.

She'd built a life for the two of them, one in which I didn't exist.

When I asked her what she'd told him about me before now, she said she'd told him the truth. That I lived in New York, that she wasn't sure where to find me.

"You don't lie to kids about stuff like that," she'd said when I stood in her office the next morning. "That's where identity crises come from—from parents not being open with their children about what happened and where their dads are."

I'd been impressed with her. But everything she did impressed me.

I knocked on the damn door, deciding to get it over with. God, I was a shark in the boardroom, I could close any fucking business deal with my eyes closed. But I was practically having a panic attack just meeting a four-year-old kid.

When the door opened, Liam stood in front of me.

"Hi," he said.

I smiled down at him. "Hi."

"You're the man from the other day," he said.

I nodded. "The one with the shoes."

He giggled. "Yeah."

"And you're Liam," I said.

He nodded again.

"Is your mom home?" I asked.

Izzy appeared at the door a moment later. She looked beautiful in a pink top and leggings that skimmed over her curves, but she also looked nervous. She offered me a smile, and invited me in.

"Try not to look at the boxes," she said apologetically. "I haven't had time to unpack."

"It's been a day, Izzy," I said. "It's okay."

She nodded, aware that I had a point. But she was a perfectionist and she always wanted everything to be just right. I liked that about her. I was drawn to the need for excellence.

"So, how do you like the place?" I asked.

They'd ended up moving in on Thursday afternoon. I'd given Izzy the afternoon off to take care of things, and she'd brought Liam home to their new place after preschool that evening.

"It's amazing!" Liam cried out and grabbed my hand. "Come see my room." He paused. "Can I show him my room, Mommy?"

Izzy laughed and nodded, and I followed Liam to his bedroom. Izzy followed behind us, but kept her distance. She was giving us space.

"You can see the pool from here!" Liam cried out. "We went to test the water yesterday. It was cold!"

I laughed and glanced at Izzy, who leaned against the wall with her arms folded over her chest, a mixture of happiness and uncertainty on her face.

Liam turned to me, his big brown eyes serious. "What are we doing today? Mommy said we should have fun."

"We absolutely should," I agreed. "I was thinking we should go to the beach."

"Yeah, the beach!" Liam cried out and Izzy laughed.

"The beach it is," she said.

It only took a few moments to get everything together. I already had swimming trunks and a towel in my car, which I went down to retrieve as Izzy changed clothes. I traded my pants for the swim trunks while Izzy packed a bag with towels and toys. When she tried to pack food, I shook my head.

"We'll eat at a restaurant. I've got it."

She looked unsure, but she nodded. After she secured Liam's car seat in my new Audi, we left. I'd decided to stay longer in LA than I'd planned, so I'd just purchased the vehicle. For now, I could remain in the hotel I was in until I figured things out with Izzy.

I drove us to Santa Monica with Liam chattering happily. He had a lot more energy now that he wasn't sick. I parked the car a couple blocks from the boardwalk, and we walked to the beach.

Once we arrived at the sand, Liam immediately ran toward the waves, but Izzy called him back to put on sunscreen. I watched as she kept him calm, carefully applying the goop to his face and shoulders, listening to his excited babbling. She really was a good mom.

"Don't go in yet," she warned him.

"Can I just dip my toes in the foam?" he begged.

She laughed and nodded. "I'm right behind you."

When he ran to the edge of the waves, Izzy pulled down her jean shorts and lifted her shirt over her head. She wore a bikini, an emerald-green little number that revealed just the right amount of her sumptuous skin. She let her fiery mane of hair loose from its bun, and it fell down her shoulders, bright red in the sunlight.

The sight of her round breasts, toned legs and curvy hips took my breath away.

When she caught me staring, she blushed.

"You look incredible," I said.

She blushed even harder. "I have to go after him."

I pulled off my shirt and followed Izzy and Liam to the water. He squealed when the waves crashed over his feet. Izzy splashed water on him, and he splashed her back, laughing uproariously.

Izzy glanced up at me, her eyes twinkling. Her gaze moved over my bare torso for a moment, lingering. Then she slapped at the waves, sending a spray of cool water to douse me.

"Hey!" I said, feigning upset.

Liam broke into laughter as I splashed Izzy in return, soaking her from head to toe.

I couldn't imagine anything more perfect. I'd gone from being a single man, fucking my way through a long string of girls whose names I'd forgotten almost before they left my place, to something approaching a family man. I was with a woman I was falling hard for, and a little boy that was adorable in every way.

And somehow, it didn't scare me. Maybe I was shell-shocked. Maybe I felt stuck in a dream and I wasn't ready for this to be real yet. But whatever it was, the day with them was perfect.

When the sun started setting and Liam complained that he was hungry, we got dressed and walked across the road to a restaurant that catered to beachgoers. We were taken to a table that overlooked the ocean, and the setting sun created splashes of orange and pink in the sky.

"This is great," Izzy said to me. "Thank you."

I nodded. "My pleasure."

"Do you want me to tell him?" she asked, taking a deep breath.

Right now? I nodded cautiously. I was nervous as hell all over again. I had no idea how he would react. But I wanted him to know.

"Liam, sweetheart," Izzy said. "Remember how I said your daddy was in New York City?"

"And you don't know how to find him," Liam echoed casually. It was clearly something they'd discussed a lot.

She grinned. "Yeah. Well, he's here now. And I finally found him."

Liam perked up. "What?"

"Liam, Carter is your father."

The boy lowered the toasted sandwich he'd been eating and looked at me with big, liquid eyes.

"Really?" he asked. "You're my daddy?" He tilted his head to the side.

"Yeah," I said. "I am."

Liam frowned for a moment, thinking about it. Then a smile spread over his face.

"That's so cool!" he said.

I laughed. "It *is* pretty cool."

Izzy took her son's hands in her own. "I didn't know where to find Carter for a long time. But when I started my new job, it turned out he owns the company. We hadn't seen each other in so long. It was a big surprise to both of us."

She glanced at me and smiled.

"So are you boyfriend and girlfriend?" he asked, looking between the two of us.

"Well—" Izzy stammered, unsure how to answer.

"We're friends," I answered, glancing at Izzy. I wasn't sure how to read her face.

"Are you going to visit us every day?" Liam asked eagerly.

"As often as I can," I promised.

Liam nodded, happy with the answer. He looked at me for a long moment, letting it all sink in. Then he kept eating as if it were all that simple. And maybe it was.

When I looked at Izzy, she looked as relieved as I felt. I smiled at her, and she returned the smile before glancing down at her food, pushing it around her plate. I looked at my sandwich, too, but I couldn't focus on eating. My mind was with Izzy and Liam. My *family*.

I wanted to do something special for her. I wanted to treat her to something she never got to do for herself, something she would never be able to do. She'd given up everything to raise Liam, and I wanted to give her something that would show her how much she meant to me. And that I saw everything she'd done, that I saw how hard she worked at giving Liam everything he needed.

Isabelle was a great mother, and I wanted her to understand that. She was a great person too, and I wanted her to know I thought that.

Everything about having her back in my life was great, and I was going to let her know—somehow—just how wonderful it was to see her again, to be with her, and to be in the position of being a parent alongside her.

It meant everything to me that she trusted me enough to let me get to know Liam.

And this was just the start of our journey.

Maybe New York could wait after all.

CHAPTER 21

ISABELLE

*I*t was Friday, a week later, and things were better than I could ever have imagined they would be. I'd gotten paid, and the extra money was more than I knew what to do with right away. I'd never had extra after paying the bills, and it was an incredible feeling to know that I'd done this—I'd managed to land a good job that would take care of my son.

But it wasn't just the job and the salary increase that made my life so much better.

Carter was in my life again. For five years, I thought I'd never lay eyes on him again. I thought Liam would never know his father. And now here Carter was, right in front of us.

The sexual tension between Carter and me was still strong. I knew we both wanted to jump into bed again, but something between us had shifted. It had become deeper, more serious, and even though we weren't technically together, it felt like he'd returned to my life to stay.

And he was in Liam's life, too.

I'd been worried about telling Liam that Carter was his

father. I hadn't known how he would take it. I didn't want to shake the foundations of his reality and make him struggle to adapt. But Liam seemed to have taken it all in his stride. He was happier than I'd seen him in a long time. My mother had commented on it too, after she'd picked Liam up for a mid-week ice cream date after preschool two days ago.

And that made me incredibly happy. All I wanted was for my son to live his best life, to have everything he needed and to have both parents dote on him the way he deserved. He was such a wonderful little soul, a blessing in my life, and if he was happy, I was happy.

I glanced at the clock, looking forward to leaving the office and getting home. I still had an hour or two left, but soon I could go back to Liam and we could enjoy the weekend in the new condo. The place was amazing—I couldn't thank Carter enough for what he'd done for us.

And I was trying to accept Carter's new role in my life, even as I factored him into Liam's life.

Carter sauntered into my office a moment later.

"Hey, beautiful," he said, and I blushed.

"Hi." I sometimes still struggled to think straight when I was around him. Carter was the guy with the X-factor. He was drop-dead gorgeous, rich, he ran a company and he was a decent person. But he had that something extra, too. That something that would make me fall head over heels for him if I wasn't careful.

Lately, I'd been wanting less and less to be careful.

"I'm going to have to ask you to stay a little later tonight," Carter said.

I frowned. "Really?" I'd been looking forward to going home, and I didn't want to disappoint Liam.

"Yeah, but not for work."

"What, then?" I asked, perking up a little.

"I want to show you something. A new… investment."

"Okay," I said. "I just need to take care of Liam, so that he doesn't sit at preschool until all hours of the night."

Carter shook his head. "I called one of your friends."

"What?" I cried out.

"Bernie, I think she said to call her. She said she'd be more than happy to pick Liam up and take care of him for a short while. She said she knows the routine and she's dying to go to your new place."

I couldn't believe it. "You're incredible."

Carter bowed from the waist.

"I just need to text her and make sure she's okay with that," I said, reaching for my phone.

He smiled a little. "You don't trust me?"

I blinked. "I do. I just have to double-check. And I have to call the preschool to let them know she'll pick him up."

He nodded. "I'll leave you to it, then."

"I can't believe Bernie is going to explore my home without me showing her around," I mused.

I'd promised my friends I would show them the place as soon as I was settled. I'd planned to have them over this weekend. June was going to be pissed that Bernie got to see the condo before her. I giggled at the idea.

"Let me know when you're ready to leave," Carter said, leaning over my desk and pecking me on the cheek.

I blushed again and he grinned at me, waggling his eyebrows before he left my office.

I struggled to focus on the last of my work. It was Friday and my mind was fried. Plus, I was curious about what Carter wanted to show me. Not to mention hot and bothered even after that quick kiss. He had a crazy effect on me. And it had been a few weeks since we'd had sex in his office. I was ready for a rematch.

I hadn't seen much action in the bedroom the past few years. I'd had a couple short-term relationships that ended up going nowhere, and the sex had been lackluster. But I'd been fine with my shop being mostly closed up. Now that Carter was back, it was a different story. I was like an addict who had managed to stay away from my drug of choice for years, but I'd been pulled back in. I was hooked all over again.

I was addicted to Carter.

Finally, I finished up and shut down my computer for the evening. I closed my door and walked to Carter's office, where he was on the phone with one of his vendors.

When he ended the call, he smiled at me.

"Ready?" he asked.

I nodded. "Ready."

We left the office together and went down to the lobby. In the elevator, Carter took my hand, intertwining our fingers. We were locked together like that until the moment just before the elevator doors slid open in the lobby.

I still wasn't sure what exactly our relationship was, or where we were headed, but that was okay by me. Slow was just what I needed, especially with how fast everything else was changing in my life. It had been five weeks since I'd started the new job and I was still reeling from all the changes so far.

I climbed into Carter's car. My car had been fixed—Carter had taken care of everything, including footing the bill. Today, I left it in the parking garage at work, and Carter said he would drive me back to retrieve it later. I was happy with the arrangement, because it meant more time with him.

He navigated through the city in his Audi. On the ride, his hand kept finding mine, his fingers lacing through mine, never stopping, playing with me. I liked the way he was touching me lately, the way he reached out to me more often, and the way he seemed never to be able to stop staring at me.

It reminded me so much of the night we'd shared so many

years ago, when we'd lingered in the café before we went to his apartment.

That reminded me of something else. Carter had never taken me to his current house. He'd always come over to our condo.

"Where do you live now?" I asked.

"What do you mean?" he asked, glancing at me.

"What do you think it means?" I asked, laughing. "I'm sure you're not back in that apartment you were in years ago, right?"

Carter grinned. "No, I'm not in that place anymore."

Before I could say anything else, he made a turn into a neighborhood. Our surroundings drew my attention.

"Where are we?" I asked.

"You know where we are," Carter said.

He was right. I *did* know where we were. It was close to the college where I'd studied art. I hadn't been here since Liam was born. It brought back a wave of nostalgia, and I looked around.

The neighborhood had changed a lot. We were surrounded by art galleries—one after the next—restaurants, and cafés. It seemed a lot more touristy than it had before, but it was easy to see that a lot of students still walked around here, probably going out on a Friday night after they'd focused on their studies all week.

I'd been keeping up with some of the artists who spent a lot of their time here, who had shows at the galleries, and my heart constricted. This was the life I could have had. This was the life I'd wanted.

If I had to look back, I wouldn't have changed anything. If I had to do it all over again, I would still have chosen to have Liam. He was the light of my life. He made everything I did worthwhile and being a parent was fulfilling in ways I never would have imagined. I loved doing everything with him.

But still, this life... I missed the part of me that used to live in this world, that used to paint and dream and look toward the future without knowing exactly where I would end up. Not caring that I didn't have a set plan.

"Here," Carter said, fiddling in his pocket and producing a set of keys.

"What's this?" I asked, taking the keys from him.

He pulled the car up in front of a building and smiled at me. "It's the keys to your new studio."

I blinked at him, not sure what he was saying. He chuckled and nodded toward the building.

"Go ahead," he said.

I climbed out of the car and Carter followed me as I walked to the door, uncertain. I unlocked the door with the keys he'd handed me, and pushed it open. A set of narrow stairs led to another floor, and I climbed them, Carter close on my heels.

When we reached the top, I looked around the large, open space and gasped.

It was an art studio, kitted with full canvases, frames, paint and supplies. A pile of sketchpads and pencils lay on a desk. Large full-length windows looked out on a perfectly manicured little yard, and when Carter flicked on the lights, they breathed magic and life into the room.

"Oh, my God," I said, turning around to face Carter. "What *is* this?"

"It's a way to make up for your lost dreams," Carter said.

I stared at him. He knew. He understood. Carter had looked at my life and seen everything I didn't say and everything I didn't do, and he *knew.*

"I don't know what to say," I said, emotions welling up inside me and tears pricking my eyes.

"You don't have to say anything," Carter said softly, his face reflecting so much of the emotion I felt.

Suddenly I could not bear it anymore. I flung my arms around his neck and pressed my lips against his. He kissed me back, and I felt his desire for me.

"Thank you," I said when I finally broke the kiss.

He pulled me back to him and kissed me again. I gave over to the warmth that radiated from his skin, to the way his arms locked around me and pulled me closer and the way his tongue slid into my mouth.

The kiss turned urgent. I had a fire at my core that needed to be fed. I needed Carter to help me with it. I needed him. I *ached* for him.

He felt the same, I could tell. The emotions spilled between us as our hands moved over each other's bodies. I unbuttoned his shirt bit by bit, my breathing intensifying as he lifted my blouse and his fingers found my bare skin.

I moaned when he grasped my breasts, pulled the cups of my bra down, tweaked my nipples and rolled them between his fingers.

He broke away from my mouth just long enough to pull my blouse over my head and drop it on the floor before he kissed me again.

I unclasped my bra and flung it to the side. I pushed Carter's now-unbuttoned shirt off his shoulders, and when we embraced again, it was skin on skin.

I loved the feel of him, the way our bodies fit perfectly together, the way his heat matched the fire in my belly.

"I need you inside me," I whispered.

A smile spread over his face.

CHAPTER 22

CARTER

*E*verything about Izzy was intoxicating. When she kissed me, I felt like I'd been drowning my whole life and finally I broke the surface, and I could breathe again. When she touched me, my skin was on fire in a way that made me feel animated, like I'd come back to life.

When she was naked, touching her was like a dream. Her skin was soft, her lips were perfect, and the way she moaned and gasped when I had my hands on her breasts and my mouth on her neck made my already-hard cock that much harder.

I wanted her so badly. I wanted to be inside of her, to feel every inch of her body, inside and out, as I slid home with every thrust.

But I didn't want to rush things. In my office that day, we hadn't had a lot of time, but tonight I wanted to take all the time we needed to do it right. Not just to fuck—although we would do that first—but to make love.

That was what I wanted with her. I wanted to erase all the years we'd lived in different cities, all the time we were supposed to be together and fate had taken us on different paths, and I wanted to be as close to her as I could get.

I dipped my head and sucked her left nipple into my mouth, my other hand kneading and caressing her right nipple. She moaned, pushing her fingers into my hair. The sounds she made, the little whimpers and gasps, made my cock twitch and throb.

I switched hands, moving my mouth to her other breast and kneading and massaging the first, and she gasped and moaned again. Her body undulated under my touch.

I wanted more. I wanted it all. I started kissing my way down her torso, but she pulled me up instead. Her brown eyes were dark and filled with lust. She kissed me again, letting me into her mouth when I slid my tongue over her lips, and while she kissed me, her hands trailed down my naked chest, my stomach, and to the belt of my pants. She undid my buckle with ease, pulled down my zipper, and pulled my cock free.

When she wrapped her fingers around my shaft, I groaned. My breath caught in my throat when she started pumping her hand up and down.

She only kept it up for a moment before she sank to her knees. She moved her eyes up to me. In that moment, she was the most incredible woman I'd come across, beautiful and perfect.

On her knees in front of me, just as I'd pictured her for a long time.

She moved her head forward and sucked my cock into her mouth. I groaned again when she took it in further, her mouth wet and slick and fantastic. I grabbed fistfuls of her fiery hair and guided her, pushing my cock deeper and deeper into her mouth, as deep as she would take it.

My balls tightened and I was dangerously close to coming.

I didn't want this to finish—not yet.

When I pulled out of her mouth, it made a popping noise. She licked her lips, and it drove me crazy.

"I need to taste you *now*, Isabelle," I growled.

I pulled her up, grabbing her hand and pulling her against me, and I kissed her. I started doing what I'd initially planned and worked my way down her body. When I reached her hips, I started working her pants and underwear down her legs. She stepped out of her clothes when they pooled around her ankles and she kneeled on the carpet in front of me. She lay back and her legs fell open for me, giving me exactly what I wanted.

For a moment, I just stared at her naked body, gloriously perfect.

Then, I dove between her legs, going for the honey. God, she tasted incredible. I lapped at her pussy, and she moaned and cried out as my tongue flicked over her clit again and again. I pushed my tongue into her, and that made her whimper and tremble. I loved that I could please her like this, that she gave herself over to the pleasure completely.

When I pushed two fingers into her, she cried out. I pumped my fingers in and out of her while I licked and sucked on her clit, and she cried out and gasped, her sounds moving to a new level.

I finger-fucked her harder, and she cried out. Her body shook, her legs trembled, and it wouldn't be long before she came undone at the seams.

Just as I thought, she bucked her hips against my face and cried out. I felt her body contract and release around my hand and she closed her legs, locking my head into place. I chuckled against her pussy and when I did, she moaned louder. She was in the throes of her orgasm and it was delicious.

I wanted to fuck her. Badly.

I pulled my fingers out, licked them clean of her juices, and sat back on my heels. I was still wearing my pants— albeit halfway down my ass—and I fiddled for my wallet. I found a condom and ripped the foil, trying to kick off my pants and roll the rubber over my cock at the same time.

When I was wrapped up and ready, I kneeled between Izzy's legs. She looked up at me with her eyes a little glazed.

"I want it," she murmured.

"What do you want?" I whispered. "Say it."

"I want your cock."

I crawled over her body and kissed her, our lips meeting, our tongues swirling around each other as my cock pushed desperately against her entrance. When I pushed into her, she cried into my mouth, and I felt her body tightly squeeze my member as she took me in.

"Fuck, being inside of you is perfect," I muttered against her lips.

"I feel the same," she gasped, and I started sliding in and out of her. Her eyes rolled back and her mouth fell open as I stroked her insides. I started slowly, sensually, moving in and out at a leisurely pace. I was teasing her, making her want more. Hell, I was making *me* want more.

But this was how I wanted it. Slow and sensual, for now. And then I wanted to fuck her brains out.

She grabbed onto my shoulders, her fingers digging into my skin and her eyes locked onto mine.

"Harder," she whispered.

And hell, I wasn't going to say no to that, was I?

I started pumping into her harder and faster. I fucked her until she cried out at every thrust and I went deeper and deeper and deeper. Her pussy was sopping wet, I could feel it even through the condom, and the way she curled her body around me with every thrust made me want more. And more. And more.

She orgasmed again. It was incredible. I was taken by how incredibly open she was, how she could give herself over entirely. She'd been like that the first time we'd been together, too. There was nothing self-conscious about her, even after she'd had a child, and I loved the way she gave herself over with complete reckless abandon.

After her second orgasm, I pulled out of her and lay on my back. She mounted me, and I lifted my hips to penetrate her once more. Isabelle rode me with her full breasts bouncing. I moved my hands from her chest to her ass. I was transfixed watching her move on me, until I couldn't hold back any longer.

I squeezed her round ass, thrusting myself into her deeper. As she reached her final climax, I released my load inside her tight walls. Our bodies merged together, our connection so close I didn't know where I ended and she began.

By the time it was all over, we were both slick with sweat, trembling, and breathing hard. I was spent after emptying myself in her, and she yawned. The third orgasm had been the one to take it all out of her.

We lay together on the carpet in the new studio.

"I think we christened the place," she said with a giggle.

"As one should," I said gravely.

She smiled at me, and we lay together in silence, enjoying the sanctity of the moment. I ran my hands over her body, tracing her perfection. I ran my fingers through her hair, over her smooth skin, relishing the feel of her.

She stared sleepily into space as we rested in the silence.

Suddenly, she rolled away from me and stood. Her naked body was glorious in the lighting of the studio. She moved toward one of the canvases and tipped her head to the side. I watched her as she studied the canvas for a moment before she picked up the paints and brushes I'd gotten for her.

I pushed myself up and watched her. She grabbed tubes of paint, squirting them one by one onto a palette and mixing the colors here and there. She worked methodically with a practiced ease that came only from experience.

She started painting on the canvas, working with sure strokes, creating an abstract image. I watched in awe as she turned from lines and random shapes into something relatable, something I could see, colors I could *feel*. She was an incredible artist. I'd never seen any of her work, I'd only known what she did.

And it was spectacular to watch.

Not to mention that she stood there, completely naked, painting as if she was the only person in the world. Her creativity was something I hadn't seen in anyone else, and it made her come to life in a way I hadn't seen before. It was like a light had gone on inside of her, and she was illuminated and glowing.

This was what she was born to do.

"You're a natural," I said. "You have more talent in your little finger than most people hope to have in their entire life."

She looked over her shoulder and it was as if she was coming back to herself. She blushed, looking embarrassed, looked back at the canvas for just a moment, and set her paints and brushes down.

When she came back to me, I pulled her tightly against me.

"I'm sorry," she said. "I just... I haven't felt like that in a long time. Inspired, you know? I just had to get it out."

I shook my head and kissed her before I answered. "Don't apologize. That's what it's here for. Enjoy yourself."

She nodded, but she didn't get up and go back to her painting. She stayed with me, and we were wrapped up in each other, clinging to each other as if this whole thing was going to disappear into thin air if we weren't careful.

This had been a good idea. I should have done this a lot sooner. I suddenly wondered why I hadn't. I had known she'd given up her art degree, that her life had taken a different turn. I'd learned as much from her file the moment Austin had given it to me.

I hadn't thought what it meant. I hadn't *understood* that what she'd given up, what she'd sacrificed to have Liam, hadn't just been a hobby or a passion. It had been a part of her. A very big part. And without it, she had to have felt so incomplete.

Well, it was never too late to set things right. I wasn't going to let anything like this happen again. She was going to be able to paint again no matter what, I would make sure of it. Slowly, I was arranging things for her so that her life could belong to her again, and so that she could take care of Liam and herself the way they both deserved.

I was so glad I was a part of their lives. I was so glad I'd come back to LA when I had.

A pang shot through my chest when I thought about New York and going back there.

After five years in the Big Apple, maybe it was time for me to move back home to California.

After business school in New York, I'd stayed there because it had been easier. I could avoid my father because we were in different cities. It was less painful to live in a city where there weren't any memories of my mom, too. Everything had seemed simpler.

Looking at it now, it looked a lot more like running away.

Well, no more. Maybe it was time to get someone else to manage the offices in New York. I could pop in there once in a while to supervise. It would be a major transition, but maybe I could swing it.

And then I could be with Liam and Izzy – the people who were starting to feel like family.

I wasn't quite ready to make a decision about it. Not yet. Things were too good with Izzy to ruin them by bringing up the subject. It was difficult to admit that I'd hidden the reality of my situation from her. Even if I'd done so with only the best intentions.

But I knew that sooner or later, reality would catch up to me.

CHAPTER 23

ISABELLE

*J*ust when I thought everything was perfect, it got even better. But everything about Carter was like that. It had been that way when I met him, too. It was one of the reasons I'd left without saying goodbye, without leaving him my number.

Because he was so perfect, it seemed too good to be true.

Except, it was true.

All of it.

And it was happening to me. The last five years had been hard. I'd worked myself half to death to make ends meet, I hadn't had a lot of time to spend with Liam and just see him grow, and I'd been worried sick I wouldn't make my rent. I'd been terrified half the time we would get evicted.

For the first time, now that Carter was in the picture, I didn't have to worry about the future. I knew that Liam would be taken care of. He would go to a good school. He would have the best education, and he would have someone else to look out for him, not just me and my mom and my friends.

He had his dad in his corner, and that was the best thing a boy could ask for.

It meant that I had a lot more free time, too. Liam went to preschool and I worked normal office hours. My mom started seeing Liam to spend time with him and not because I needed someone to take care of him. I even had a girls' nights with my friends where the three of us could go out for a glass of wine or two, and I didn't have to worry so much about finding more work, about money, about having Liam looked after.

Whenever I could sneak away, I was at my studio.

It was glorious to paint again. Giving it up had been hard, but my life had become so busy with Liam and everything I'd had to do to look after him, I hadn't had time to miss it all that much.

Now that I was painting again, I realized just how much I'd missed it. I realized how much it was a part of me, a part I hadn't seen in a long, long time. Putting a brush to canvas, mixing paints and bringing an image to life brought me such a sense of peace and fulfillment. I didn't know how to explain it to someone.

I knew Carter wouldn't understand how it *felt* but he understood that I felt something *special* when I painted, and I was forever grateful that he'd given me the studio. Sometimes, I had to pinch myself to remind myself that it was real.

I hadn't finished my art degree and I was sad about that. But just because I hadn't finished didn't mean that I couldn't paint. My fingers itched to hold a paintbrush. And when I painted, all the worries and tension fell away until I was light as air.

Until I was flying.

Liam loved coming with me to the studio. At first, I'd been worried that he was going to be bored and I'd have to get a babysitter or something, and that would stop me from coming here as often as I liked. But very quickly I realized that whatever artistic talent I had in me, he had it, too. Whenever I came to the studio to paint, Liam wanted to come with me. He often sat with a large page in front of him, scribbling or finger painting, creating art just as I was.

Sometimes, Carter came with us, too, and it was the three of us in the studio. When I was younger and studying, I'd always wanted to be alone when I was creating my art. I wanted to be left in peace, feeling like anyone who insisted on sitting with me was intruding in a world I wanted to go to alone. But when Liam and Carter were with me, I didn't feel that way about it. I didn't feel like I was being held back or dragged down.

They were welcome in my world. In fact, I felt almost lonely when they *weren't* with me.

It was a Saturday at the end of the next month. Carter and I had only been seeing each other again for two months now, but it felt like he'd been a part of my life—and Liam's—from the start. It was crazy how it felt like we fit together, like this was always how it was meant to be.

"Pardon the mess," I said to Carter when we walked up the stairs. Liam ran ahead and immediately jumped onto the pile of pillows I'd brought in for him to play on. There was a stack of books next to the pile, a kids' easel and a few jars of finger paints and crayons scattered around. "I haven't really taken the time to clean up."

The rest of the studio was just as messy, with half-painted canvases in one corner, completed works stacked off to the side, and paint tins and tubes everywhere. Brushes stood in jars, and my coveralls lay on the floor in the corner where I'd kicked them off.

When Carter looked around, he chuckled.

"This is perfect," he said. "I would have been worried if it didn't look like this."

"Look what I painted," Liam said and Carter walked to Liam's corner, where he made all the right sounds of being impressed about his work. He glanced up at me, eyebrows raised, and he looked like he was genuinely impressed.

"He has a lot of talent," Carter said to me.

"Grandma says I get it from Mommy because she has no talent in her old bones," Liam said.

I laughed and shook my head, already starting to mix paints for the new painting I'd been thinking about.

"I'd like to meet your grandma one day," Carter said. "She sounds like a wise lady."

"She knows *everything*," Liam said.

I smiled and glanced at Carter. I wanted to introduce him to my mom. All in good time. Right now, we were just taking things one day at a time. My mom knew all about him, and so did my friends, but I was keeping Carter to myself for now.

I started painting, getting lost in the colors and the brush strokes, feeling the therapy that came with it as it spread through my body and took away all my worries and fears and anything that made me feel restless. This was my happy place. Not just here at the studio, painting, but with Liam and Carter here, too.

After a while of working, I felt eyes on me. When I turned to look at Carter, he was taking photos of my work. He took photos of the canvas I was working on before he walked to the stack of completed paintings and worked his way through them.

"What are you doing?" I asked.

"Taking photos of your work," he said matter-of-factly. "Your work is good, Izzy."

I shrugged one shoulder, keeping the brush steady in my hand. "I don't know about that."

"Are you kidding me?" Carter asked. "Your use of color is

fantastic. It's mesmerizing." He lifted a large canvas I'd painted of a woman with a butterfly over her head, candle-light that colored one-half of her face orange, and strokes of color that ran down the other side. It was a little more whim-sical than usual, but I loved the way it had come out.

"I never finished my studies, Carter," I said. "I can paint, but I'm not going to be a world-renowned artist or anything. I'm okay with that, too. I mean, once upon a time, that was what I wanted. But I'm happy with what I have."

Carter shook his head, working through my other canvases. I watched him carefully, my attention divided between him and the art I was working on.

"I think you're taking photos of my work so you can brag to your friends," I teased.

Carter chuckled. "Would that be so bad? Your work deserves to be seen."

Liam watched Carter rummage through my canvases.

"Do your friends want to see my art, too?" he asked.

"Of course," Carter said with a chuckle. "I must take photos!"

He walked to Liam and I smiled as he made a fuss of taking photos of his crayon squiggles and his finger paint splotches.

"I'm serious though, Izzy," Carter said when he was done taking photos of Liam's pictures and started tickling Liam instead. My boy squealed and giggled and I smiled. "You really should consider showing your stuff to people."

"Like who?" I asked. I walked to the table and squirted more paint onto my palette.

"Someone who's connected in the art world," Carter said.

I shook my head, mixing the right colors for what I needed. "I don't think so. Right now, it's just a hobby. I'm happy with it this way, too. I have everything I need. I have you here, and Liam, and I get to paint. What else could a woman want?"

Carter nodded, but I could see he didn't agree with me. But I wasn't in that space anymore. My life had changed direction. I had a child to raise now. I had to focus on work, I had to focus on raising Liam. Painting wasn't my whole life anymore. And that was fine by me. I had a direction and I was following it.

I hadn't been able to do art until now, but thanks to Carter, things had changed. I appreciated that he'd brought my art back into my life, but I wasn't going to try push for something bigger, something more than I had now.

I hadn't been this happy in a long time. Not since I had gotten pregnant. I loved Liam, but I hadn't had the time to really be happy.

Now, I had Liam and Carter and art and that was all I needed in life—this right here. That was it. I didn't need someone to tell me my art was good. I didn't need to end up in galleries and sell my paintings for thousands of dollars. I just wanted Liam to be safe and happy. I wanted stability.

I wanted Carter to stick around.

It was getting late, and the boys were patient with me, waiting for me to finish up. When I finally did, we collected our things and headed toward the condo.

"What are we going to do for supper?" Carter asked me as he drove.

"Pizza!" Liam cried out from the back seat.

I laughed. "I don't know. I think we should—"

"I'm okay with pizza," Carter said. "And a movie. What do you guys think?"

"I want to watch a movie!" Liam agreed, and I laughed in my defeat.

Pizza and a movie it was. A perfect little family date.

A few blocks from the studio, Carter stopped to get gas.

Liam needed to go use the restroom, so the two of us headed inside the gas station while Carter filled the tank. Liam chattered happily about what movies we could watch the whole time.

When we emerged from the building, I froze.

Carter was talking to a woman standing near his car. A *beautiful* woman wearing a short, form-fitting dress and a trendy hat atop honey-blonde hair she twirled between her fingers.

My insides clenched as we walked toward them. Carter looked up at me and smiled.

"Izzy, hey," he said to me. "This is Madeline. She's an old friend from school. Guess it's a good night to get gas on Sunset Boulevard."

"Hi," I said. The woman gave me a weak smile, said hello, then turned her adoring gaze back to Carter. She didn't even look at Liam.

"Anyway, Carter, nice to see you again," she said to him warmly. "Hope to run into you again sometime."

"Have a good night," he said in a neutral voice.

She sauntered off toward her BMW parked nearby, and Carter closed the lid on his gas tank. I got Liam buckled up in his car-seat, then I stood up and turned to Carter once more.

He glanced at me. "Ready to go?"

I tried to keep my voice even. "An old friend, Carter?"

"That's right," he said. "An ancient friend. I haven't seen Madeline since my college days. She was a business major like me."

I studied him for a moment, my eyes narrowing. "She was awfully flirtatious."

He laughed and kissed me on the cheek. "You don't have anything to worry about, Izzy. I don't think she was flirting. If she was, I wasn't flirting back because I have no interest in her. It was just a coincidence that she was getting gas here at the same time."

I let out an exhale as he pulled me in for a tight hug.

"I'm crazy about you, silly," he said.

"Okay, let's go home," I said.

He didn't seem to be lying, so I decided to let it go. I didn't have any reason not to trust Carter, and I didn't like feeling jealous.We arrived home, called for a pizza delivery, and Liam chose *Cars* for us to watch.

"Ah, a classic," Carter said when the movie started playing and the three of us were cuddled up on the couch, plates loaded with pizza on our laps. Liam was squashed between the two of us and watching the movie intently.

"My favorite," I agreed. I'd seen *Cars* so many times I could recite the entire movie.

Before the end of the movie, Liam fell asleep with his head leaning against Carter. My heart melted when I saw him like that.

"I should get him to bed," I said.

"Let me," Carter said, and he carefully wriggled out from underneath Liam before hoisting him onto his shoulder. He carried Liam to his bedroom and I watched them go, thinking that this was what I'd wanted my whole life. My boy and his daddy together, the three of us a family.

Nothing could be more perfect than this moment.

But somewhere deep inside, I feared this wonderful life would come to an end sooner or later. I didn't know how, but part of me was waiting for the other shoe to drop.

Was Carter afraid to make a commitment? He'd told Liam we were just friends, and he hadn't told the woman at the gas station who I was to him, either. Just introduced me by my name.

But he'd done so much for me, been so generous. I was grateful. How could I not trust him after all that?

Maybe it was just hard for him to put a label on our relationship. After all, things between us were still pretty new. I told myself I was just being paranoid.

I'd been so accustomed to everything falling apart that I almost expected disaster. Maybe this thing with Carter would be different, though.

But a tiny voice inside me wondered how long I had until my luck ran out.

CHAPTER 24

CARTER

*I*sabelle was quickly becoming my everything. I knew that it had only been a few short weeks since we'd started seeing each other, and even less time since I'd met Liam and fully understood what was going on in Izzy's life, and learning that I was more intimately involved with her than I could ever have hoped for.

But I knew how I felt about her. I knew that no matter what we'd been through, and how different our lives had been, fate had aligned us and we were together now.

And I wanted her to know how important she was to me.

"So, tell me again," Austin said when we sat at the bar, drinking together. It had been a while since we'd hung out—I was incredibly busy with work and with Izzy, and Austin was doing his thing, running his side of the company.

"Come on, man, it's not a big deal," I said, sipping my beer.

"Are you fucking kidding me? It *is* a big deal. Not only you telling me you want to commit to one woman—something I *never* thought I'd hear you say—but you're telling me you're a father, too? It's a lot to wrap my mind around."

I nodded. "I know. Trust me. It's a lot to wrap my mind around, too. But the truth is I'm serious about her. And I want to be in her life. Both of their lives. The kid is adorable, man. And he deserves to have his dad around."

"So..." Austin started, but he didn't finish his sentence.

"So, what?" I asked.

"What does this mean for New York?" Austin asked carefully. "I'm assuming that means you're not going back?"

Shit, I'd forgotten about New York. Again. It just seemed to slip from my mind. Or maybe I'd pushed it out of my mind. How could I think about leaving LA when Izzy and Liam were here?

"I'll figure it out," I said.

"You're going to have to figure *something* out if you're not planning on going back."

I hesitated. It wasn't that I didn't want to go back—I loved New York. I had a whole life there. But I had a life here now, too. How was I supposed to choose? My mind ran in circles. Sometimes I thought about telling Izzy I wasn't here to stay, and asking her to come back with me. But that would uproot her and Liam completely.

Sometimes I thought about staying in LA. But what about everything I'd built in New York? What about my offices and my employees and everything else? I could get someone to manage the office the way I did here, but it was harder to leave something behind I'd put so much into.

Austin had been running the offices here from the start. I hadn't been a part of it except for taking care of things over the phone whenever I needed to jump in. It wasn't the same as building the whole place up from scratch.

But I was being an idiot, wasn't I? I was falling for Izzy. And she was the mother of my child. I loved spending time with the two of them. Was I really going to be an asshole and give all that up?

"I'm going to figure something out," I finally said to Austin. "But first, I'm going to treat Izzy, give her something special to let her know how much she means to me."

Austin grinned at me and waggled his eyebrows.

I laughed. "Yeah, we fuck all the time. That's not any more special than usual."

Austin shook his head and downed the last of his beer before he lifted his hand and waved for another.

I kept to my plan. The next weekend, I arrived at Izzy's place with a surprise.

"I've arranged for you and your mom to have a spa day," I announced.

"What?" Izzy asked, looking surprised.

"You haven't had time off, and you haven't had time to spend together. So, I think you should kick back, relax, and get a full body workup."

Izzy laughed. "You can't call it that!"

"I can, and I just did," I said with a chuckle. "Manicure, pedicure, facials, massages, saunas and soaks, it's all included, plus lunch. You can do whatever you feel like, even just sit and talk in the tranquil gardens if that's what you want."

Izzy shook her head. "That sounds incredible. But... what about Liam?"

"I'll take care of him, if that's okay with you. It'll give us a chance to bond."

Liam appeared around Izzy's legs the moment I said it.

"Really?" he asked. "Do I get to go with Carter?"

He still called me Carter, not Daddy. We would work on that. We had time.

"Can you take that on?" she asked me doubtfully.

"Of course," I promised. "He'll be in capable hands, Izzy."

She thought it over for a moment. She'd seen me with him, the way I was always careful and attentive with him. I knew the world could be dangerous, and I never let him out of my sight.

"Would you like that, Liam?" Izzy asked.

"Oh, yes!" he cried out. "That would be wicked cool!"

I laughed. Izzy smiled and nodded, beaming with excitement. "Okay, then. You can spend the day with Carter while Grandma and I have a girls' day."

Liam cheered and ran to his room to pack things to take along with him.

"Thank you," Izzy said to me. "This means more than you know."

"Of course," I said and kissed her. "I want you to be able to have a good time and spend time with the people you love."

"Where are you going to take him?" she asked.

I lowered my voice. "I was thinking of the theme park he noticed in Santa Monica. He said he loves the Ferris wheel."

She grinned. "He *would* love that. But are you sure you can handle him for the whole day? He's quite a handful."

"No sweat," I said. "You don't have to worry."

"Okay. Just take good care of my baby, okay?"

"Of course I will. He'll be back here safe with you in a few hours."

"And you remember how to work his car-seat?" she asked.

"Absolutely," I assured her. I'd bought a new car-seat to keep in my Audi for the times he rode with me.

She nodded. "Okay, I know you'll take care of him. And he's going to have so much fun with you. He gets tired of boring old me."

I laughed. "No one could ever call you boring, babe."

I watched as she grabbed her things. She gave Liam a kiss goodbye, then me, and she left a few minutes later. Soon it was just me and Liam.

"What are we doing to do?" he asked, coming out of his room with a backpack on his back and bright eyes.

"Anything you feel like doing," I said. "Where should we start?"

"We should go buy toys!" Liam cried out.

I laughed. "Okay. One toy. And then we can go to the theme park and go on the rides a little. What do you say?"

Liam agreed wholeheartedly, and we walked out to the car together.

It was great hanging out with him—two guys out on the town. I'd been a little nervous to spend time with him alone. Izzy had been around every time we'd been together to fill the silences, to take care of him, and to mediate our relationship. I'd thought it was going to be hard to find something to talk to Liam about—I barely knew him and I didn't know all that much about kids and their interests.

But Liam took care of my dilemma for me. He talked nonstop. And about everything and anything. He told me about the Ninja Turtles, which he'd only just discovered. He talked about *Cars*, which we'd watched just the other night, and then he went on to tell me how he wasn't really into that anymore because he was a big boy now. Although I knew that he didn't want to sleep unless his *Cars* comforter was on his bed.

He asked questions about everything we saw, and the way he looked at the world wasn't only amusing, it was also contagious. Having kids wasn't about looking after someone else as much as it was about looking at the world through new eyes. I'd never thought about what it would mean to be a father, aside from being a provider.

But with Liam, I was starting to see the world on a different level. Liam asked questions about everything around us. He wanted to know why the sky was blue, and how birds could fly, and why airplanes didn't have to flap their wings. He wanted to know how burgers were made when we had them, he wanted to know how his curly fries got curly, and he asked if there really were tomatoes in ketchup because the colors weren't the same. Just like his artist mother, he noticed slight differences in the two shades of red.

He talked and asked questions, and time flew faster than I'd thought it would.

After the toy store, theme park, and lunch, I was running out of ideas for what to do with him. We'd been all over town and I'd spared no expense, but he was starting to fall quiet and he looked tired.

I wondered if it was a good idea to take him home for a nap. But then I had another idea.

"Hey," I said to Liam. "How about we go visit my dad?"

"Is he nice?" Liam asked.

"He is."

"Okay," Liam said. He thought about it for a moment before he added, "If you're my dad, does that make him my grandpa?"

I nodded. "It sure does."

Liam nodded, satisfied with the answer, and we drove to my dad's house.

I was suddenly excited. I wasn't sure why—my dad and I hadn't been on very good terms for a long time. But this was Liam, my son. And I was excited about introducing him to my dad.

When we arrived at my dad's place—a little outside the city—my dad seemed wary. He shook my hand as asked me how I was, politely keeping his distance. But when Liam hopped out of the car and came around, he looked up at him with those big brown eyes that looked just like Izzy's, and my dad melted.

"And who's this young man?" he asked, kneeling in front of Liam.

"I'm Liam." He said it just the way he'd said it to me.

"Yeah? It's nice to meet you, Liam. I'm—"

"You're my grandpa," Liam said proudly.

My dad glanced up at me and I tensed for just a moment. How would my dad respond to Liam's claim? He was always so proper, so serious about doing the right thing and treating people the right way, about respect and dues, and all the rest of it.

But his face split into a wide grin.

"You're right. I am. We should have milk and cookies. Do you like cookies?"

"Who doesn't?" Liam asked.

"Liam," I said sternly.

He glanced at me before he looked back at my dad. "I like cookies. Please can I have some?"

My dad laughed and nodded and we walked into the house together.

Walking into my childhood home brought a wave of nostalgia with it that nearly knocked me off my feet. It had been nearly a decade since I'd been here last. I'd avoided coming to see my dad here so that I wouldn't have to think about my mom. The pain had always been too great. But now, being back here, it didn't hurt the way I'd thought it would.

It felt a lot like coming home *should* feel.

We walked to the kitchen and my dad made coffee with the single-serve coffee machine. He showed Liam how it worked, letting him help put the pods in, and after he made our cups of coffee, Liam got a cup of hot chocolate with his cookies instead of a glass of milk.

I watched my dad with Liam. It was sweet to see how he was acting around him. He was kind and patient, and he clearly enjoyed being with the boy. He could be a good grandfather.

A pang shot through my chest when I remember the family we'd once been. My dad had been like this with me before my mom had died, and I missed that. Maybe Dad and I would be able to bond again. Maybe we could fix the break that had happened between us.

All in good time, though. I wasn't going to hope for anything more than what we were getting today.

We carried our cups and plates of cookies to the patio where we sat in the sun, chatting and laughing. I let go of the time, I stopped thinking about work, I just enjoyed the moment, drinking in the wonderful time I was having with my father and my son.

By the time we were getting ready to go, the sun had already set. We'd stayed for supper, rather than just leaving after the snack. In the car on the way to the condo, Liam yawned at least three times. His head started to nod as he was dozing off, but I kept him awake with questions, making him talk to me, until we were at the house. The last thing I wanted to do was to ruin his bedtime the first time I took him out. I wanted Izzy to see that I was a good father, that I could do this.

When we pulled up in front of the complex, Izzy's door flew open and she came down the steps. Her face was riddled with concern, and her eyes were filled with fear.

"Mommy!" Liam cried out and ran to her. She grabbed onto him, hugging him fiercely.

"Did you have a good time, honey?" she asked after she glared at me.

My jaw tightened. What the hell had gotten into her?

"It was great!" Liam cried out and happily chatted with her, telling her everything as we all walked into the house. She got him bathed and ready for bed while I put on a kettle

181

of tea in the kitchen. Whatever was bugging her could be taken care of, I was sure.

I listened to the harmony of their voices as they talked in the bedroom, and finally, Izzy appeared in the living room after she'd put Liam to bed.

"I made you tea," I said. "I thought coffee might keep us up tonight."

"Thank you," she said tightly, but she didn't move to pick up her cup from where I'd put it on the coffee table.

"Do you want to tell me what's bothering you?" I asked.

She glared at me. "Do you want to tell me why I haven't heard from you all day?"

I frowned. "What do you mean?"

"I mean, *I haven't heard from you all day.*"

I blinked at her. "Yeah, I wanted to leave you and your mom alone so you could have a good time."

"And not check in with me once about Liam?" she asked. "I tried to call you fifty times! I was just about to contact the police, Carter. I thought maybe there had been an accident or... " Her voice broke, and she choked back a sob. "I didn't know what to think."

I frowned and took my phone out of my pocket. It was on silent.

Damn. Nice move, Jacobs.

I hadn't heard the calls and texts come through. And there had been a *lot* from Izzy.

"I'm sorry," I said to her. "That was stupid of me. But Liam's fine. We were having a great time. You can see how happy he is."

Izzy shook her head and sank onto the couch. Then she burst into tears.

CHAPTER 25

ISABELLE

What the hell had he been thinking, taking my son away from me and not checking in with me one single time? I'd trusted him with my whole world, letting him walk away with the one thing that meant the most to me.

And I hadn't heard from him all day. At first, I'd been just a little worried. It wasn't how I knew Carter—he usually always answered his phone. Hell, his entire business relied on it. When my calls kept going to voicemail, my mind had jumped from worried sick that something had happened to them, to terrified that Carter had taken my son from me and left for good.

I knew it was ridiculous of me to think that, but it had happened to people before—how many stories were there about the father stealing the children away and the mother having no idea where they were? It was the first time Carter had had Liam and I hadn't been there.

When I burst into tears, I felt like an idiot for crying. But the whole day had been terrible. I'd had a great time with my mom at first. But I'd soon gotten so worried I hadn't been able to enjoy it, and I'd left the spa early in a frenzy.

I covered my face with my hands.

"Hey," Carter said gently and sat down next to me. He put one hand on my leg. "What's wrong?"

I glared at him through tear-filled eyes. "Do you seriously not know the answer to that question?" I asked.

Carter looked shocked at my reaction for a moment. "What?"

"You walk in here like I haven't been frantically calling your phone for the past six hours at least, and you don't think there's something wrong with that?"

"I missed the calls, Iz. I'm sorry."

"That's not enough!" I cried out. "I don't trust *anyone* to take Liam from me. Only my mom, my two closest friends, or the preschool has him when he's not in my sight. It wasn't easy for me to let him go with you. But I told myself it would be fine. I'm supposed to let you spend time with him, right? Because you have a legal claim to him. But you can't do this to me, Carter. You can't make my life hell like this."

Carter shook his head, looking confused and irritated.

"I gave you a day to just relax and have a good time with your mom, and now suddenly I'm the bad guy. Yeah, you're right, I didn't let you know where we were and what we were doing, but he was with *me*, Izzy. I'm his dad."

"I know that," Izzy snapped. "But that still doesn't give you the right to not tell me. I'm his *mom*. It's been me, all this time. Just me, no one else—"

"Look," Carter said, interrupting me. He shifted a little on the couch, moving away from me. He was angry now. "I know you're his mom and you've done it all alone. I told you I was impressed with how well you've managed. But you can't use that against me when you're upset about something."

"I'm not trying to use it against you."

"Then why did you bring it up? I know I wasn't there, but that wasn't my fault. And I'm here now."

I shook my head. "I brought it up because until now, it's just been me. I've been the only one to look after him, the only one responsible. It was my job to keep him safe, and I did that. I need to know where he is at all times."

Carter sighed and shook his head. "Look, I get it. You're always the one taking care of everything. But it doesn't have to be like that anymore. You're not alone in this now. I missed a few calls, and I'm sorry about that, but he was fine. We were having a good time. It's not such a big deal."

My throat tightened.

I was ready to accept what he was saying right up to the point where he said it wasn't a big deal. That made me fume.

He was minimizing my fears, telling me they didn't matter.

"You don't get it, Carter," I said, standing and taking a few steps away before turning around to face him. "It *is* a big deal. That's my son in there. I need to know he's safe. It's your job to let me know he's safe when he's in your care."

"It's my job to keep him safe too," Carter said. "You're not the only one. I made a mistake, okay? God, just let it go."

I saw red for a moment. Just let it go?

I was trying to talk to him, to tell him what it was like for me. I was trying to show him my side. And he was telling me to just let it go.

Well, I wasn't just going to let it go.

I shook my head and pressed my fingers against my forehead. I put my other hand on my hip. My mind was racing, my heart beat in my throat, and I couldn't think straight.

Carter had taken my son away from me. It hadn't been for very long, but it had scared the living shit out of me. I'd feared something had happened to them.

I couldn't face that kind of fear ever again.

And I couldn't do this.

"I don't think this is going to work out," I said.

Carter frowned at me. "What are you saying?"

"We gave it a shot, we tried to figure it out. But it's not working. I don't think we should do this anymore."

"Izzy…" His voice sounded as unsure as he looked. "Are you breaking up with me?"

I started to say yes, but he'd made it pretty clear he wasn't my boyfriend. We were spending time together and sleeping together, but that didn't mean anything in the long run. And I was pretty sure he didn't *want* it to be long term.

"I would," I said. "But we're not officially together, are we?"

"What are you talking about?" Carter asked, looking alarmed.

"I mean, you never actually asked me to be your girl-friend. You don't tell people we're together. This thing between us has been great, but we're not exclusive, you never told me you wanted more with me than… this."

Carter was fluctuating between confused and angry.

"What the hell do you think I've been doing here all this time if what we are doing doesn't mean anything to me?"

"I never said it didn't mean anything," I said. I lifted my chin a little higher, determined to stick to my guns, to not let Carter derail me, no matter how difficult this was. "But whatever this is between us, I don't want it anymore."

Inside, I was shocked at my own words. I was lying to both of us, and I hated myself for it. But I had to end it to protect Liam—and myself.

I did want Carter. I wanted all of it. But I couldn't share Liam. Not like this—not in a way that cut me out of the equation completely. It wasn't supposed to be like this. I needed to take care of us. That had been my job from the start—taking care of Liam, keeping him safe, making ends meet, keeping our heads above water. It didn't always look the same. Sometimes I took care of us financially by juggling jobs and doing the right thing so that Liam had the life he deserved. Or as close to it as I could get.

And sometimes, it was emotional. Sometimes, taking care of us meant taking care of *me*, so that I could do all the other things. There was a reason I hadn't really looked for another man to fill the gap Carter had left behind. There was a reason I hadn't put my own heart on the line again. It was so that I could do right by Liam. I hadn't had time to date in so long, and I hadn't wanted to.

Now that I had been with Carter again, I'd had a taste of something delicious. But I still had to prioritize my son.

And what had happened today was a harsh reminder that things weren't as easy as I'd hoped.

And that was okay. I had to do the right thing.

Carter stood and came to me. "Don't do this, Izzy. Let's work it out."

"How do you want to work it out? This is a big deal to me, and it's not to you. I can't change your mind about that, but I can make up my own."

He groaned. "It's a couple of hours, Isabelle. It's nothing!"

I sighed. "That's just the thing, Carter. You might think it's nothing, but to a mother who thinks her child has gone missing, it's an eternity. And the fact that you don't think that kind of agony is a big deal is exactly why this can't work."

Carter was angry now, the confusion gone completely.

"I can't believe you're doing this," he snapped. "One small thing goes wrong, and you're willing to throw it all out of the window."

"It's not just one thing," I said meekly.

"You're making a mistake, Izzy," Carter said. "You're walking out on the best thing that's ever happened to us."

I didn't answer him. Inside, I was breaking. I knew he was right, that this was great. I knew I was running at the first sign of trouble. But I'd been terrified something was going to go wrong, that something was going to shatter the illusion of this new life, this fantasy that I was chasing. I'd been waiting for the house of cards to come tumbling down at any moment.

And here it was. The moment when I realized that the happy ending I'd thought I might have found had just been an illusion after all. Soon, I'd have to return to the grind, to getting life right for just the two of us.

Was this ever meant to be in the long run? I had no idea. All I knew was that after everything I'd been through, after everything I'd done and everything I'd sacrificed to get here, I didn't have what it took to go on an emotional roller coaster ride, too.

And that was exactly what today had been.

"I'm sorry," I said to Carter. My voice was void of emotion, despite the hurricane that raged in my chest. My tone was even, my face carefully expressionless.

"You don't look very sorry," Carter said, his face closing off too.

I hated that he was withdrawing from me, but that was what I was doing. I was pushing him away. It was safer that way.

"I guess that's my cue then, huh?" Carter said. "After everything, this is how it ends."

I didn't answer him. What was I going to say?

I wanted to ask him to stay. I wanted to take it all back, to say I'd been wrong. That I couldn't bear to see him walk out that door. A voice inside me was screaming, begging me to stop this train wreck.

But I knew if he didn't leave now, he'd just leave later. If I pushed him away now, it would save me more pain down the line.

"I'm leaving your place," Carter said, turning at the door. "But I'm not the one walking out on this relationship. I'm not the one running away. You're doing that. Then again... this is how the whole thing started, isn't it? I guess I should be lucky you didn't leave this time while I was asleep."

He opened the door and closed it behind him, leaving his words to hang in the air. My chest ached, my throat closed, and I struggled to breathe. His words hit me like punches, and I sank onto the couch, fresh tears rolling over my cheeks.

The part about me leaving him the first time stung. We hadn't been together back then. It had been a mistake, but how could I have known how things would end up? He was angry now, trying to get back at me.

And I supposed I deserved it. His heart was broken, just like mine.

I covered my face with my hands and sobbed. I let out all the pain and fear. The day was filled with panic that had quickly turned to misery.

I was left with an ache that was worse than anything I'd felt before.

I sat there for a long time, staring at the wall. Finally, I took a deep breath and swallowed down my tears. I wasn't going to allow myself any more time to fall apart. I had a son to look after, a career that I needed to somehow pursue, and a life I needed to stop from coming undone at the seams. I started flicking off lights as I walked to the bedroom, ready to get to bed.

This condo didn't belong to us, I thought as I walked. The studio didn't belong to me. Nothing I had now belonged to me, it belonged to Carter. I was going to lose it soon.

I had to start looking for a new place to stay, and I had to jump the gun and find a new job so that I was gone before Carter could fire me.

Reality hurt. Having to think like that hurt. But I had to be realistic. There was no reason Carter was going to let me keep it all after I'd kicked him out like that. I wasn't going to expect anything else from him.

When I lay in the darkness, I tried to figure out a plan of action. Instead, my mind kept drifting back to the way he'd looked at me, the shock, the pain, and then the quiet resignation when he'd realized I was serious.

For a moment, fear clutched at my throat. What if I'd made a mistake?

But no, I'd done what was needed. And it didn't matter now, anyway. What was done was done. The last thing I was going to do was crawl to him with my tail between my legs. It had never been my style.

I had caused this. I had asked for it. And now I was going to do my best to make it work. It wasn't the first time I'd been on my own, needing to work it out. I'd done it before, I could do it again.

The few weeks in between were a nice little holiday, a fantasy, a break. It was going to be a hard crash back to reality, but I was going to figure it out.

I could do this.

There just wasn't any other way.

CHAPTER 26

CARTER

*W*hat the fuck was I still doing here in LA?

Isabelle wanted nothing to do with me, so I might as well pack up my bags and go back to New York. The original plan had never been for my stay to be permanent, anyway. I'd been in LA much longer than I'd counted on.

If she could just up and leave, then so could I.

But damn it, I didn't want to leave things the way they were. I didn't want to go without saying goodbye, and I sure as shit didn't have the taste for my life before Isabelle anymore. Not after I'd felt what it could be like. Not after I'd had a taste of real happiness.

What the hell was I supposed to do?

When I walked into Austin's office on Monday morning, I was in a shit mood. I'd just been dumped, and even though I hadn't done anything I really thought was wrong, I felt like the dick in this tale. And that made me even more pissed off.

"What's up with you?" Austin asked when I sat in one of the leather armchairs he had facing his desk. "You look like shit."

"Thanks," I said sarcastically. "I'm going back to New York."

Austin blinked at me. "That's a sudden decision."

"Since when?" I asked. "I wasn't supposed to be here this long anyway. I'm way overdue."

"Yeah… and what about Isabelle?"

I snorted. "What about her?"

"Oh," Austin said. Understanding. At least, he thought he understood. But I didn't even know exactly what had happened, so how the hell could he fully understand what was going on?

"Is this really what you want to do?" he asked carefully.

"Why the hell wouldn't it be?" I snapped. "I ran the New York offices for years without you questioning my motives."

"That's true," Austin said. "But that was before you met someone you're serious about. And what about the kid?"

I rolled my eyes. "I'll send him cash, I'm not a deadbeat."

"That sounds like a very shitty thing to do," Austin pointed out.

"Did I ask your fucking opinion?" I sneered.

Austin held up his hands, palms toward me. "Hey, I'm just saying. No need to take your bad mood out on me."

This was the reason Austin and I were still friends. He gave it to me just as it was. He didn't sugarcoat anything, and he was one of the few people who wasn't afraid of me when I was in a shit mood like this. He'd always been a hell of a friend.

"Well, there *is* a lot of work to take care of," Austin said. "What with the launch and the new expansion of our products, keeping the New York office running smoothly is crucial."

I nodded. That was what I wanted to hear. I liked that my business was doing well. That was the only part of this whole story that made sense to me. It was the one thing I was good at. I knew what to expect, I could bend things to go my way, and I made a lot of money.

Business was simple.

"I'll get the word out that you're going, then," Austin said.

He watched me, trying to gauge my reaction to his statement. I wasn't going to have one. It was settled, then. I was going to leave. Maybe, when I was back in New York, I would be able to forget about everything that had happened with Izzy and Liam. I could forget about the life I'd started creating here without realizing that I was putting down roots.

I'd have to tell myself that Liam was better off without me. That I would have made a terrible dad, just like my own father. I was doing the kid a favor by staying away. Sure, it broke my heart to leave him behind, but I'd have to live with that pain.

I would go back to being the cold-hearted son of a bitch I'd been in New York, sleeping with whoever I wanted and living my life without getting attached. Because getting attached just fucked everything up.

The way I felt now, and what had happened with Izzy, was just proof of that. Damn it! I was so fucking pissed off that I'd let it go this far. That I'd let myself fall for her.

No matter how right it had felt, how *perfect*, this pain was ridiculous. It was exactly the pain I'd been trying to avoid.

After I lost my mom, I'd learned what real pain and loss felt like. Then I'd lost Isabelle five years ago. The first woman I'd really felt like I could fall for.

Never again, I had told myself. I hadn't been ready for more of that kind of suffering.

And look at what I'd done to myself all over again.

I left Austin's office. I didn't go to Izzy's office to talk to her. I didn't need her to tell me again that she didn't want to see me. I didn't need her to rub salt into my wounds. I already felt fucking sorry for myself and even though I knew it was pathetic, I wasn't going to go there.

I didn't even know if she'd come into the office today. Maybe, maybe not. Whatever. I didn't care. I walked to my office and sat down behind my desk, set on finalizing all the details before I left for New York again.

It was better this way.

I managed to lose myself in my work. It was a relief to just forget for a while. I pushed Izzy and Liam far away, to the back of my mind, and focused on making sure that my company was doing well. The LA headquarters ran smoothly with Austin at the helm, and as soon as I was back in New York, the same would be true for that branch.

And I would be happy again.

Although, without analyzing it too much, I knew that was a load of shit. Because I wasn't going to be happy there, was I?

And I wouldn't be in Liam's life.

Austin had been right—skipping town now just because I was pissed off and saying that I would send the kid money was really a deadbeat thing to do.

Just because Izzy and I didn't see eye to eye and weren't going to have a relationship—God, it hurt to admit that— didn't mean that I couldn't have a relationship with my son. He didn't deserve me skipping out on him, too. He deserved for me to be around. I'd pushed Izzy to tell him who I was, so I had to step up now and be a man.

Otherwise, what had happened between me and my father would happen between me and Liam, and that wasn't right. A boy had to have his father around. My dad hadn't left town—I'd been the one to do that eventually—but he'd become so emotionally distant, he might as well have left.

And that wasn't going to be me.

The day I'd spent with Liam had been incredible. I'd felt

like we were getting closer, like I'd gotten to know him better. And right now, our conversations didn't amount to anything more than who the best Ninja Turtle was, and speculating about how the sky really just reflected the ocean. But one day, there would be more to talk about. And I wanted the line between us to be open and clear so that I could have a real relationship with him one day. So that he could have what I never did with my dad.

So that we could be close.

How was I going to do that if I lived in New York? The answer: I wasn't.

The concerns about Liam brought me to Izzy all over again. Because seeing my son would mean that I would have to see her, too. Maybe not for long periods of time on end, but long enough that I would know that she wasn't mine anymore. And that was going to hurt like hell.

Did I want that—did I want awkward, strained conversations about what time he last ate and when he went to bed the night before, with undercurrents and so much left unsaid, only to turn around and walk away again? Did I want to have nothing in common with her other than the child we had together?

The answer to that was just as simple. I didn't want that. All I wanted was for the three of us to be a family again.

Izzy was right when she'd told me we weren't exclusive. I hadn't asked her to officially be my girlfriend. I guess a part of me had been terrified of what it would mean to be in a committed relationship. A part of me had been terrified to put it into words, because then I would have scared myself out of it and I would have run away.

But a part of me had also imagined that it didn't matter if I didn't put it into words, because it made sense. I'd thought that having a child together and spending almost every waking moment away from the office together would show that we were meant to be together and that we were committed to each other.

That was on me. I should have done something about it.

And then there was that awful encounter with Madeline at the gas station. I should have introduced Izzy to her as my girlfriend. But I'd panicked when I'd run into Madeline. She was someone I'd dated briefly years ago—before I'd ever met Izzy. And I had zero interest in Madeline anymore.

Hell, when I laid eyes on Isabelle in my office that day weeks ago, every other woman might as well have fallen off the face of the Earth.

But still, I'd been nervous I'd handle it wrong, that Izzy would get suspicious when she saw Madeline talking to me. And I'd botched the whole thing. I knew it had planted seeds of doubt in Izzy's mind.

The more I thought about it, the more I realized what an asshole I'd been all along. I shouldn't have dismissed her anger about missing her calls that day with Liam. She'd been scared, and I hadn't been there for her. Instead, I'd told her that it didn't matter.

I still didn't completely understand what she'd been so upset about, but I did know that I should have listened. I should have tried to see it from her side.

And I shouldn't have let her leave at the first sign of trouble. I should have fought for her. I knew she was scared, and she had every right to be. She'd been doing this alone, giving up on every dream she had to raise our child when I'd been chasing my own dreams without a care in the world. She was the one who had always picked up the pieces alone, and it was easy to imagine why she believed she had to do it again.

She wasn't the only one at fault here—I was, too. And this time, I wasn't going to let her get away.

I stood up from my desk, determined to find Izzy and make it right. I marched to her office and knocked on the door. When there was no answer, I opened the door. The office was immaculate, with everything in its place. And all her personal items were gone.

I frowned and walked to the staff break room where I found Felicity eating her lunch.

"Where's Izzy?" I asked.

Felicity looked at me with wide eyes and swallowed the food she'd been chewing on.

"Didn't you hear?" she asked.

I narrowed my eyes at her. "Hear what?"

Felicity glanced around her as if she was hoping for backup but she was alone, and I was serious about getting an answer. I glared at her until she swallowed hard, this time swallowing nerves instead of food.

"She quit," she said in a small voice.

"What?" I cried out and turned on my heel, storming out of the break room.

I made my way to Austin's office, where he was bent over his desk going over documents.

"She quit?" I cried out. "Why the hell wasn't I informed of that?"

Austin frowned at me. "Because I'm in charge of HR and it's not your department," he said. "And I thought you were leaving."

"Why the fuck is she gone?"

Austin gave me a look that suggested I should have known the answer to that question. When I didn't respond to his look, he took a deep breath and let it out slowly.

"I told you I would announce your leaving. Just after I did, she came and offered her resignation, effective immediately."

I blinked at him. What the hell was going on? How could she just up and leave like that? And what about Liam and taking care of him? It was ridiculous that she was doing something so spontaneous. She couldn't afford to do that.

But if Austin had mentioned I was going back to New York, she knew that I hadn't come here to stay.

God, that would only have made everything sound so much worse.

I turned around and left Austin's office.

"Where are you going?" he asked.

I didn't answer him. The truth was, I wasn't completely sure where I was going. All I knew was that I couldn't keep doing this. I couldn't keep playing this game where I ran away from my emotions. At some point, I was going to have to turn around and face the music.

In a way, I'd already done that with my dad, spending time with him again when we hadn't been on good terms for years. I could do that with other areas of my life, too. I just had to close my eyes and jump.

Scary as it was.

Because loss hurt like hell, but this time, I was at least partly responsible for it. When I was a kid and my mom passed away, there hadn't been anything I could do. But I was a grown-ass man now, and I could do something about this situation.

It was time for me to step up and be a man.

CHAPTER 27

ISABELLE

I had to do it. The moment I'd heard Carter was leaving, I couldn't stay at the company one minute longer.

It had been a stupid move, in terms of taking care of Liam. I knew that. I was going to have to find another job and I doubted I was going to find something as good as I'd had it at Appetite. But Austin had told me that he'd give me a good reference, and I had a bit more experience when it came to design and marketing now. Not enough to really put on my resume, but enough to try to convince someone that I could be an asset, that I had a foundation that could be built on with the right guidance.

I would find something.

I couldn't have stayed. Carter was leaving, which meant I wouldn't see him again, but that didn't mean that I wouldn't be reminded of him every step of the way when I worked in *his* offices at *his* company, essentially working for *him,* although Austin would became my new manager as soon as Carter was gone.

It was just too much to handle.

Bernie was at the school where she taught, and I was relieved to see the kids outside on break. The timing couldn't be better. When I found her in the staff room, she looked surprised to see me. After we walked out to the private courtyard, meant for the teachers only, we sat down on a little bench.

"Do you want something to eat?" she asked. "I have an extra yogurt."

I shook my head. I couldn't think about food at a time like this.

"What's wrong, Iz?" Bernie asked. "You look scared to death."

"I am," I admitted and raked my hair out of my face with a trembling hand. "I feel like everything's happening all over again. I feel like I'm in a life I don't know how to handle, just like when I learned I was pregnant."

"What do you mean?" Bernie asked.

I let my breath out with a shudder and told her what had happened. That I'd told Carter to leave. And that he was literally *leaving*. Going to the other side of the country.

"I don't get it," Bernie said after I told her everything, stopping in the middle of my tale to snivel and sob. "Why did you end it?"

"Because I can't have something that will fail, Bernie. I can't do this. I can't... get hurt again."

Bernie nodded. "I get that. I mean, I think I do... Ryan really screwed you over and just after that, Carter happened and you got pregnant. But... the way I see it, you're already hurting *now*."

She was right, of course. I *was* hurting now. More than I'd ever thought I would. I cared about Carter. Our relationship —or whatever it was—had been moving toward something. But I'd been convincing myself that it wasn't serious. I'd been telling myself it was for Liam's sake, not mine. I'd been telling myself I was fine, I wouldn't fall for him. I hadn't for one minute allowed myself to believe that Carter had crept into my heart, and now that I'd tried to dig him out, he'd taken a part of my heart with him.

"I don't know how to do this," I said softly. "I don't know how to share parenting. I've done this alone for so long, I don't know how to give Liam up. Even just a part of him. I was so scared when Carter kept him longer than he should have. I thought he was taking Liam away from me for good."

"But he brought him back," Bernie said.

I nodded. Carter *had* brought him back. I'd freaked out, and it had turned out to be okay. But I had been so scared and angry. And he'd dismissed my feelings.

"I've fought tooth and nail to make it work," I said to Bernie. "I did everything I could to make sure he was okay. And then Carter swooped in out of nowhere and suddenly everything was paid for and taken care of and it was almost like I wasn't needed anymore. Carter doesn't *need* me, Bernie."

Bernie shook her head. "You can't see it that way. You don't *need* him, either. You've been doing just fine."

I gave her a pointed look.

"Okay, maybe not fine. It was hard and there were down days. But you got through it. You survived it. But just because you don't *need* someone by your side doesn't mean that it's not nice to have someone. And he did what he was supposed to do—he took care of the two of you."

I wanted to argue with her, but she was right. Carter hadn't done anything terribly wrong. Not really. He hadn't heard me out, or tried to see my side, and he'd brought Liam back a little late. I just hadn't been able to reach him.

But in the grand scheme of things, it could have been so much worse.

I'd freaked out and acted from a place of fear, when I

should have calmed down and talked to Carter about it. I should have told him what I needed from him for future reference, instead of telling him I didn't want a future with him at all.

He'd only been doing this dad thing a month. I'd been a parent for almost five years.

God, I felt like a such a fool.

"You should talk to him," Bernie said.

"I can't," I said. "He's leaving. Going back to New York."

Bernie gaped at me. "Are you serious?"

I shrugged.

"This is déjà freaking vu if I've ever seen it," Bernie said. "Is this *Groundhog Day,* where Bill Murray lives the same day over and over?"

I let out a laugh that came from nowhere. The whole thing was so bizarre. It *was* a repeat of the past, Bernie was right. But this time, I had Carter's number. And surely, he would keep in contact with Liam.

"I'm angry that he's leaving," I said.

"Why?"

"Because I didn't know that he wasn't here for good. I didn't know that the whole thing was temporary for him. He never told me he doesn't actually live in LA. And I never thought to ask because I assumed he was just... around. Indefinitely."

"So, now he's going? After *you* broke up with him? How dare he." She rolled her eyes.

"Don't say it's my fault he's leaving," I said.

Bernie shrugged. "Maybe he was going to stay for the two of you, Izzy. Have you thought about that?"

I shook my head. Maybe she was right.

"I should go," I said.

"I need to get back to class, too," Bernie said, glancing at her watch. "Izzy, I know you're hurting. I know this is scary. I know you have a thick skin and that you can do it on your own. But just because you don't need someone to take care of you doesn't mean that you shouldn't have someone. And just because Carter makes mistakes doesn't mean he doesn't love you back."

"Love me back?" I asked.

Bernie nodded. "It doesn't take a rocket scientist to see that you're head over heels for the guy, Izzy."

I bit my lip. I doubted Carter cared about me so much that he loved me.

"I'm so sorry it worked out this way," Bernie said. "I wish I could make things better for you. You've had such a rough ride."

I hugged my friend. "You're doing more than you know by just being there for me," I said. "Thank you for listening."

"Always," Bernie said.

A bell sounded and that was my cue to leave. Break time was over.

Where was I going to go now? I wasn't sure. I had to find a new job, so I would probably go home and start sending out resumes. Then I was going to pick Liam up from preschool. Maybe we could go to the park and get ice cream. Just to distract the both of us.

When I got home, I started searching online for a job. Being back here—looking for something in the online classi-fieds—was nauseating. I'd loved having a stable job, loved not having to look for new work and rely on freelance money. I'd loved not needing to rely on others to come through for me rather than doing it by myself.

But staying at Appetite would have been a mistake. I'd wondered why they'd hired me with so little experience. Carter had pushed me into a position I knew nothing about and even though I'd done my best to learn and figure it out as

I went along, I hadn't known what I was doing. Especially not at first.

I knew now why all that had happened. Carter had pulled some strings. He'd probably hired me so that he could get into my pants again. And it had worked.

I was going to find something else. I was a survivor. I always had been. I was just going to keep powering on, and one day, something was going to give. I just had to stop thinking about Carter, stop thinking about my broken heart and the fact that it was probably my fault it was broken in the first place.

I had to do what was best for Liam.

When I went to pick up Liam from preschool, his eyes were bright and his cheeks flushed. He chattered about his friends and what they'd learned in class all the way home. It was good to hear him so cheerful, and his chatting distracted me from my own thoughts. I listened intently, gasped in all the right places, asked him questions and laughed at his jokes. He was growing up, becoming a wonderful little being, and I loved the journey. I loved being there every step of the way.

That made me think about Carter, who wasn't going to be there for the journey.

A pang shot into my chest, but I studiously ignored it and turned my attention back to Liam.

When we arrived at the condo and opened the front door, Liam ran inside.

"When is Carter coming?" he asked.

"He's not coming today," I said.

Liam's face fell and he dropped his bag on the floor. "But I want to see him."

"I know, but I think he's busy," I said. "Pick that up and take it to your room, please."

"Can I call him?" Liam asked.

My heart twisted. This was harder than I thought it was going to be.

"He's at work right now, sweetheart. Take your bag to your room."

Liam huffed and did as I asked. He was back a moment later. I was making him a sandwich at the kitchen counter and he held onto the counter, tilting his head to look up at me. "When am I going to see him?" he asked. "When am I going to see my dad?"

When he said that, my heart constricted and tears stung my eyes. What was I going to say to him?

"We'll have to see when he's not so busy, honey," I finally said. I didn't know what else I could say. "He has a lot of work to take care of right now."

"Grown-ups are always working," Liam said with a dramatic sigh, and I smiled. But the smile disappeared again when Liam walked away from me, and the sadness took over again.

Liam ate his sandwich in front of the TV. He watched a new Ninja Turtles cartoon and I cleaned up a bit until my phone pinged with a message. It was from Carter. My heart beat in my throat.

The condo and studio are yours, no strings attached. Stay safe.

I stared at the message. My ears started ringing. He was giving me the condo and the studio? I'd thought I would have to move. And I didn't think I'd get to keep any of my painting equipment.

But how *could* I keep any of this, after I'd pushed Carter away like a fool?

I felt another lump in my throat. Carter was being a nice guy about this. More than nice. And now he was leaving.

I had made the worst mistake of my life.

CHAPTER 28

CARTER

*M*y flight was booked and I was ready to leave in the morning. Unlike the last time I left LA, I didn't have an apartment to vacate, or furniture to take care of. I only had my luggage at the hotel, and that was it.

The other thing that was different was that I wasn't leaving without seeing Izzy again. I knew she was pissed at me, and that she didn't want to see me again, but I had to talk to her at least one more time. Not only to arrange a custody agreement and child support for Liam, but because I couldn't leave her without saying goodbye.

Not this time.

We met at a café. Not the same café where she'd worked all those years ago—that would have been far too cliché—but nevertheless, a sense of déjà vu hit me when I walked in and she was sitting there, waiting at one of the tables.

She was so fucking beautiful, for a moment, a lump rose in my throat and it was hard to think that I was going to have to say goodbye to her. She was doodling on a napkin, sketching something, and her hands were splattered with paint.

This was what I loved about her so much—she saw the world in a different way. She looked at everything through lenses that no one else possessed and it was only through her art that I could see what she saw. She was unique. She was creative. She was incredible.

And she was slipping through my fingers.

This was my last chance to get her to accept me in her life, to try again.

When she looked up and saw me, her face tensed.

"Hi," she said.

"Hi."

Her body was rigid and she chewed on her bottom lip as I sat down. She was nervous. She was trying so damn hard to keep it together, but under her mask I could see that she felt like I did—that she was falling apart.

It made me ache. I wanted to protect her. I wanted to keep her safe. I didn't want her to push me away, to have to do it all alone again. I wanted to take her in my arms and ward off the difficulties that life threw at her so that she would be okay.

"How is Liam?" I asked.

"He's okay," Izzy said. "He misses you."

"I miss him, too."

She nodded slowly. "So, since you're going to be on the other side of the country... how do you want to do this? He's too young to fly unaccompanied and I can't go with him to see you."

"I know," I said. "I'll come to see him. And Isabelle, thank you for agreeing to let me be in his life. Especially after I dropped the ball the other day."

She nodded.

I want to stay. I wanted to tell her that. I wanted to shout it out so that she could understand. I wanted her to be my life. I wanted both of them.

"What are we going to do about major holidays?" she asked. "You're not going to fly here for every one of them, are you?"

"I will," I said. "Whatever it takes."

She stared at me, and I couldn't read her expression.

"I don't want it to end like this," I blurted out. "I don't want it to end between us."

She still didn't show anything. Her features were still blank, tightly controlled. "You weren't going to stay, though, were you? You were here visiting from New York. And you never told me."

"I know," I said. "I should have told you. I guess I was waiting to see how things went with us. The more I got to know you and Liam, the less I even considered moving back to New York. I wanted to stay here. I still do."

She shook her head. "It's just hard to believe that you intended to stay here with us when you were living in a hotel all this time. That was what you were doing, right? That's why we never visited your place?" She took a shuddering breath. "I thought you were just trying to make it easier for us, coming to our place all the time."

That was exactly what I'd been trying to do, but she wasn't going to see it that way.

"I'm sorry I didn't tell you where I was that day," I said. "I don't always understand what it means to be a father, but if you'll let me, I'll learn."

She turned her head toward the window without answering me, and I could see the shimmer of tears in her eyes. What was she so upset about? That I was trying to get her to reconsider? Or that she wanted this too? She was so difficult to read sometimes.

"Izzy," I said, putting my hand on hers. "I want to be a part of your life. Yours and Liam's. I don't want to be on the other side of the country. I want to be with you."

"I don't know how to do this," she whispered.

I wanted to tell her that I didn't either, and that we could figure it all out together, but my phone rang, cutting me off. I frowned and took it out of my pocket.

"It's Jonah," I said to her.

"Who?"

I shook my head. "This will only take a minute."

Jonah was one of my oldest friends, and he was in the art business. He had a lot of connections. The night I'd taken photos of all Izzy's canvases, I'd sent a few of the images to him to take a look.

He'd said he would look at the paintings, but it was a tough world to compete in. I'd figured it wouldn't amount to anything. I hadn't thought I would hear anything from him again.

"Are you still in contact with the artist you sent me?" Jonah asked.

I looked up at Izzy. "I am."

"I have a gallery interested in hosting her. They want to do an exhibit. How can they get in contact with her?"

"I'll send you her contact details right now," I said, looking at Izzy. She frowned.

"Thanks, man. I'll get them to call her right away."

We ended the call.

"What was that?" Izzy asked.

"That was a friend of mine who has contacts in the art world. He hobnobs with collectors and gallery owners," I said. "I sent him your work."

"You what?"

"I told you it's good, Izzy."

"But you had no right to do that! It's personal. You should have asked."

"And you would have said no."

"Because I'm not that good!"

209

I shook my head. "Jonah doesn't agree. He sent it to a gallery, and they are interested in a solo exhibit. They want to showcase your work. I'm sending him your contact details." I sent her contact card to Jonah as we spoke. When I looked up, Izzy was staring at me with her mouth open and her eyes wide.

"Are you serious?" she asked. Her voice was thin, like she wasn't sure she could believe what she was hearing.

"I'm serious," I said. "I told you how talented you are. You should show your art to people."

She shook her head, still looking like she didn't believe me.

"This is…"

"This is amazing!" I finished her sentence for her. "You can make a living out of this if you want to, Izzy, you just need the right connections. You just need a break. And this might just be your big break."

"Oh, my God," Izzy said, the news finally sinking in. "A solo exhibit?"

"All your work, all your own," I said, nodding.

She stared at me for a moment, and then she threw her arms around my neck, bumping against the table so hard it scraped across the floor.

"Oh, my God," she muttered again, burying her head in my shoulder. "Are you never going to stop doing things for me?"

I closed my arms around her body, relishing her closeness.

"I love you, Izzy," I said. "I don't ever want to stop doing things for you."

She pulled away from me and studied my face, her eyes twinkling. "What did you say?"

"I said I love you."

"But... you're leaving." Her voice broke on the last word, as if it pained her to say it.

I shook my head. "Not if you want me to stay. You broke it off, Iz. Not me. I want to be with you. Officially."

She withdrew her arms, looking unsure of herself again.

"How can I be sure this is going to work?" she asked.

Her eyes locked on mine, and I took her small hands in mine.

"Because I love you, Isabelle. And no matter what, I want to make it work."

Tears sprung to her eyes. "I love you, too, Carter. I love you so much."

My heart soared. Those were the words I wanted to hear.

"I'm so sorry I pushed you away," she said. "I screwed up the other day."

"It's okay," I said. "We both did. I should have answered your calls."

She shook her head. "It's not okay what I did, though. I was terrified of losing Liam. I freaked out. And... I guess I'm scared to have a relationship with you, Carter. I'm scared of being hurt. Of losing everything all over again." She sniffed and wiped a tear away. "I guess I'm just a big scaredy cat."

I cupped her cheek. Tears spilled out of her eyes and I thumbed them away.

"I know you're scared," I said. "But we'll take this one step at a time. Together. You won't have to do it all alone anymore. I'm here now, and I want to do this with you. Be my girlfriend?"

She nodded, smiling through her tears. "That's all I wanted to be since I met you the very first time."

I smiled and pulled her closer, planting a kiss full on her mouth. She melted against me, kissing me back.

A waiter appeared, and I realized we hadn't even ordered

anything. "What can I get you?" he asked when we broke the kiss.

I looked at Izzy, who was staring at me through her tears, smiling, looking like everything had just become right in the world.

"What are you having?" I asked.

"I'll have a happily ever after," she said.

I chuckled and ordered us two coffees before I kissed her again. "Done," I said.

This was it. This was what I'd been missing for so long. For years I'd been breaking myself for my company. I'd met woman after woman and promptly forgotten them. I'd been searching all over, and I hadn't been able to find something that filled the hollow space inside me.

Now I knew what I'd been missing. It had been Izzy all along. We were destined to be together since the moment I'd met her. Nothing else had been good enough to fill the gap she'd left behind.

I took her hand and interlinked our fingers.

"This is only the start of our journey together, babe," I said. "It's going to be a hell of a ride."

She nodded and smiled at me, the tears drying up. "I can't wait for our adventure. I missed you."

"I missed you, too."

"I'm glad you didn't wait five years before you decided to see me again," she said. "If you left without insisting on seeing me, it could well have been that long."

I shook my head. "Not that long. I would have lasted about a day in New York. Then I would have been back here, knocking on your door, convincing you to give me another chance."

She giggled. "I'm glad we didn't lose that day, then."

"Me too," I said. "The commute all the way to New York

and back, just to end up where I started... it would be such a waste of time when I could spend it kissing you."

I pulled her tightly against me.

"Carter," she whispered.

I looked at her.

"A solo exhibit!"

I laughed and planted a kiss in her hair. God, I loved this woman more than I could say, and having her in my life was what I needed. For the first time since I'd met her, I felt truly and perfectly complete.

"You make me so happy," she murmured. "And Liam will be thrilled to see you."

I squeezed her hand. "I can't wait to see the little man again."

Our coffee arrived, and we sat together. Instead of discussing a custody arrangement, we talked about a bright future together.

CHAPTER 29

ISABELLE

I stood in front of the gallery, my stomach twisted in a knot of nerves. My cocktail dress hugged my form snugly, and the chill of the evening danced on my bare arms and shoulders. I'd pinned my hair up into an elegant chignon.

"You're going to be great," Carter said, coming up behind me.

"Oh, God," I said, spinning around to face him. "What if they hate it?"

"They won't," he said. "They'll love it."

I shook my hands, trying to shake out the nerves. Carter had been supportive since the moment I'd gotten the exhibition. He'd helped take care of Liam, often taking him out or spending time with him at the studio over the past few months as I finished one painting after another on the same theme for the exhibition. The title of the exhibit was 'Life in Colors' and it was a series of paintings of people—people I knew and people I didn't—in colors that weren't usually used. They bordered on abstract, which I had thought was a very free-spirited approach and would be frowned upon, but apparently the gallery owners loved it.

And here we were. The exhibit was starting soon. Inside, my paintings adorned the white walls of the gallery. Waiters in white shirts and black waistcoats were armed with silver trays and flutes of champagne, music floated from the speakers above, and everything looked like it belonged in a movie.

"I have something for you," Carter said.

He held out a flat black box. When I opened it, there was a diamond necklace inside.

"Oh," I breathed, nervous to touch it, it looked so delicate.

"It's a congratulatory gift."

He took it out and stepped around me, putting it around my neck and fastening it at the back. The necklace was cool against my neck. I pressed my fingers against it.

"Thank you," I said.

Carter kissed me before he glanced toward the greeter who stood at the doors that opened up onto the street. "Our first guests are here."

I turned to look and watched as the guests streamed in, moving through the gallery, looking at my art. My heart beat in my throat, and I felt strangely exposed. This was the first time anyone who wasn't a friend or family member had seen my art. Other than the gallery owners, of course. I watched them nervously. What if they hated it? What if they left because it sucked?

I watched for signs. Downturned mouths, heads shaking, half-empty glasses of champagne returned so that they could leave as soon as possible.

Instead, I saw the opposite. Nods of approval. Smiles. Pointing and waving, talking among each other. They were enjoying it. Was it possible that they liked it?

"They love it," Carter said, his mouth close to my ear, as if he'd read my mind. "You're incredible. Your work is fantastic."

"You're biased," I said with a blush.

"They're not," Carter said, nodding at the growing crowd.

And he was right. They didn't know me at all. And yet, they loved the work. It looked like they were really enjoying the evening. The waiters floated between the guests with their trays of champagne and canapes. Carter took two flutes of champagne for us from a tray nearby and handed me one.

"You deserve to let your hair down," he said.

I absently touched my updo and he grinned at me. I sipped the champagne and it was amazing, the bubbles fizzing through my veins.

It was impossible to believe this was really happening. This was a dream that I'd had for years and years when I was a teenager, and I'd had to put it all on hold when I'd gotten pregnant. For five years, I hadn't thought about it again, because it was too painful to think about what I'd given up. I loved Liam with all my heart and would do it again and again if that was what I had to do for him, but I'd still mourned what I'd lost.

And now, thanks to Carter, it was happening. I was living my dream. My paintings were on the walls of a reputable gallery. They had been advertised for months. The people who walked through the doors were complete strangers to me. They'd come because they thought my art was worth their time.

When I looked at Carter, my heart was near bursting. He was such an incredible man. He had made all of this happen for me. He'd swooped into our lives out of nowhere, and he'd turned it all around. He'd saved us.

I had been holding on. I'd been keeping us afloat, our heads above water. But Carter had been the life raft, pulling us out of the ocean so that we weren't just surviving anymore, we were *living*.

And he was a part of our lives just as I'd always wanted.

It had been a few months since he'd moved back to LA permanently, and he saw Liam all the time. His apartment was a penthouse suite that looked out over the city, and Liam loved visiting him, looking at the cars and houses from high above, pointing out fun things to see.

I loved visiting him there, too. Not only because spending time with him was amazing, but because he'd made an effort to have a room with toys for Liam, and we could stay over whenever we wanted. We weren't living together yet, but that would come.

I didn't want things to move too fast for Liam's sake. At least, that was how I'd felt at first. But we were past the point of no return—Liam and I both. He was crazy about Carter, and I had to admit, so was I. But he was here, and we were moving forward. The rest was up to him.

I hadn't worked in graphic design since Carter had moved to LA permanently. I'd wanted to go back to Appetite, or find something else, but Carter had insisted that I start painting full-time. He had the rest covered, he'd said. I'd been reluctant—it was hard to step back when I'd done it all for so long. But when Carter had insisted and I started doing it, it was such an incredible, freeing feeling that I agreed to keep doing it.

"I can't believe this!" June said, coming up to me with Bernie at her side. We all hugged each other and Carter took a step back, grinning at my friends who completely enveloped me. "I've never seen you paint like this. It's a whole new level!"

"It's just like what I've always done," I said with a laugh.

I'd been nervous for my friends to see my new paintings for the first time.

"No, it's not," Bernie said, agreeing with June. "You were good back then, but this... Were you sneakily painting at night instead of sleeping all those years while you were super mom?"

I blushed and shook my head. "I just..." I looked at the paintings. "I just painted what I felt."

I glanced at Carter, who was smiling at me. He was the reason all of this was happening, but he was also the reason everything I painted came out the way it did. I was happy. Happier than I'd ever been. And it translated into my work.

"We're going to look around, but you're really killing this," June said, kissing me on both cheeks before pulling me into another hug. "You're a star!"

I laughed, and my two friends continued on, looking at my work.

"It's because of you," I told Carter. "I'm happy, so my work is the way it should be."

"I'm just as happy, but I can't paint for shit," Carter joked.

I laughed.

Slowly, the exhibit died down until only a handful of people were left. Mr. and Mrs. Greene, the gallery owners, came to me.

"What a successful night, Isabelle!" Mrs. Greene said. "You did wonderfully. The paintings are a great success! And you have sales!"

"What?" I asked, feeling lightheaded.

"That's right," Mr. Greene said. "Look." He handed me a printed list of paintings that had all been bought.

I swayed on my feet, pressing my hand against my head. "This is almost all of them."

Mr. and Mrs. Greene both nodded at me with big smiles. I frowned and looked at Carter.

"Did you do this?" I asked.

He gasped. "What?"

"Did you buy them?" I asked.

He shook his head. "No, no, no. This is all you, sweetheart. The paintings sold because they're incredible and for no other reason."

"They're reputable buyers, too," Mrs. Greene assured me.

I couldn't believe it. My heart was racing. My head was spinning. If my paintings sold, it meant I was a professional artist. And that I could make money from doing what I loved.

The gallery owners walked off, leaving me alone with my love.

"Oh, Carter," I breathed.

He grinned.

"I told you," he said.

"I didn't believe it."

"You should listen to me more often," Carter said with a wink. "I didn't buy a single of those paintings. But I did buy you something else."

He took another small black box out of his pocket.

I glanced at him, unsure. "Carter, what is this?"

He went down on one knee, and suddenly I realized what was happening.

"Isabelle Taylor, you're an amazing woman. You make my heart sing. I love you more than I ever thought possible. Will you marry me?"

I clasped my hands to my mouth, tears springing to my eyes.

"I thought we were taking it slow," I whispered.

"I'm over taking it slow. I love you, and I want to be with you for the rest of my life."

Tears rolled over my cheeks. "Yes, Carter Jacobs. I'd love to marry you."

He smiled and stood. The few guests still remaining applauded, and I felt self-conscious. But Carter slid the ring onto my finger, and the diamonds matched the necklace he'd given me earlier.

When the ring was on my finger, I pulled him to me and kissed him.

"Thank you," I said when we pulled apart.

"For what?"

"Fighting for us. Not letting me go."

"My love, anyone who lets a gem like you go is a fool."

I smiled. He kissed me again, and I was happier than I'd ever thought I could be. The fairy tale was complete. My life was officially perfect.

I couldn't wait to get home to Liam. My mom was babysitting him so that we could attend the exhibit, and I was excited to tell her the good news. And to tell Liam that his mother and his father were getting married.

As we drove home, Carter reached for my hand.

"When do you want to do it?" I asked.

"Get married?"

I nodded.

He thought about it for a moment.

"A few months from now," he said. "Not so long that I have to wait forever to make you Mrs. Jacobs, but long enough to plan an extravagant wedding for the world to be in awe of."

I giggled. "You don't have to keep giving me the whole world, you know," I said. "I'm happy with something small and modest."

"I know," Carter said. "And I love that about you. Your priorities are straight. But I want to spoil you, and you deserve a big wedding. You deserve everything in life that makes you happy, and more. And we're going to do this right."

I smiled and he lifted my hand to his mouth, pressing his lips against my knuckles. I sighed contentedly. No matter how I'd imagined my life to be—even before I'd had Liam—I could never have imagined it like this. Carter made me feel joy I'd never even dreamed possible.

I'd lost him twice, and the pain had been unbearable. But all that was wiped away now. From now on, we were together, totally committed and devoted to each other. And only happiness lay ahead.

EPILOGUE

CARTER

I stood at the bar with Austin, drinking the most expensive whiskey they had behind the counter. We sipped it slowly, savoring the taste and our surroundings.

"I don't know how you got in here," Austin said. "This venue is incredible."

I nodded, looking around. It was one of the biggest, swankiest art galleries in LA, and I'd managed to convince the owners to let us use it as a wedding venue.

"Do you think she'll like it?" I asked.

"She'll love it," Austin said.

Of course, Izzy knew this gallery. She'd been here a hundred times at least. But she didn't know that I'd gotten it for us for our wedding. I'd roped in June and Bernie to help me hide it from her. She thought we were getting married at a second-rate ballroom. I'd even paid off the manager to pretend we were using it. Izzy was going to be thrilled when she found out we were getting married at her first choice.

The rest of it was easy. June took care of all the arrangements when it came to flowers, music, cake, and all the rest of it, and Appetite took care of the gourmet food we would be serving. It was easy to hide the venue from Izzy.

Now, it was an hour before we were getting married, and Austin and I were having a drink to celebrate. The wedding wasn't going to be a big one—we didn't have a huge entourage or a ton of guests. But the right people were here. My dad, Izzy's mom, a few of our close friends and colleagues. A few members of the press had been invited too, so that it could be broadcast across LA. But that was not because of me and my riches. It was because of Izzy and her art.

In the months after the exhibit, she had exploded into a star almost overnight. She was the new sensation, the name on everyone's lips. Her art was in such high demand, everything she painted sold—portraits, landscapes, and abstract paintings. She had a waiting list as long as her arm with buyers who wanted what she painted next, and it was incredible to see her at work.

She was wonderful.

"Let's get up there," Austin said. "It's time to get cracking."

I threw back the last of my whiskey and nodded. "Let's do it."

We walked through the gallery to where chairs had been set up to face the front of the room—a large oil painting Izzy particularly loved was the backdrop against which we were getting married.

The guests filled in, the priest joined us, and I shook hands with our guests and nodded, making small talk. My stomach was tight with nerves, but I wasn't panicked. I was anxious to get married so that Izzy could be my wife.

Finally, she arrived. The limousine slid past the tall windows, and a moment later, the music started from a grand piano I'd had brought in specially.

June walked in first. Liam walked next to her, wearing a

cute little tux and beaming at me. He held a box with two rings in it, and he looked like he felt important to have this job.

When he stood next to me, I ruffled his hair, then smoothed it back down for the pictures. "You're a champion," I whispered to him.

"Thanks, Dad."

He smiled up at me, his grin looking a lot like mine. My heart filled, just as it did every time he called me that. He'd started referring to me as *Dad* just before he and Izzy moved in with me a few months ago.

Bernie followed next, smiling at everyone, looking excited. She winked at me before she joined June.

And then came Izzy, and she was breathtaking. I stared at her as she looked around in amazement, and then her eyes locked on mine. Her dress was incredible, and her jewelry, and her makeup. Everything was perfect. When her eyes met mine, she smiled and I waited for her to come to me.

Her mother walked down the aisle with her, and she kissed me on the cheek before handing Izzy over to me.

"Take good care of her, Carter," her mom said, patting me on the shoulder.

Izzy giggled and looped her arm through mine. We faced the front.

"You look great," she whispered.

"You are breathtaking," I answered.

"So... the gallery, huh?" she said. "Sneaky."

"Just for you, babe."

She smiled and the ceremony started, followed by the vows.

We'd written our own. I turned to face Izzy, and took a piece of paper from my pocket where I'd jotted them down. A moment later, I put it back again. I didn't need to be reminded of how I felt about her.

"Isabelle, when I met you, I thought you were the most incredible woman I'd ever seen," I said. "Not only were you gorgeous, but the way you looked at life was beautiful. We only had a brief encounter before you slipped away. But now that I found you again, I'm holding onto you forever. Isabelle Taylor, in a world that was monochromatic, you brought so much color. You live your life with such inspiring passion. You make every day brighter, you touch the world in such a unique way, and you bring a smile to my face whenever you're in the room. You inspire me to be the best man I can be. I love you more than you'll ever know, and I will do everything to take care of you and Liam for the rest of my life."

Izzy's eyes were filled with tears, and she sniffed. June handed her a tissue over her shoulder and Izzy brushed the tears away without smudging her makeup.

"Carter Jacobs," she started. "When I met you, I thought the world stopped turning. You were my oxygen when I could hardly breathe. And then, I thought I'd never see you again. But now I stand in front of you, ready to become your wife. And I'm the happiest woman alive. You bring me so much joy that my heart can hardly contain it. You fill me with a peace and happiness that I've never known before. Carter, I promise to always trust you, because you've shown me the depths of your heart. I promise to believe in you, just as you've never failed to believe in me. And I promise I will love and cherish you for all the days of my life."

She held my gaze, and the moment was perfect.

Liam stepped forward with the rings, and everyone ahhed at how cute he was. The priest said the last few things, and we each said our 'I dos' before we slipped the rings onto each other's fingers.

Izzy kneeled and hugged Liam, and I ruffled his hair again.

"A perfect family," Izzy said.

I nearly welled up at that, too.

The rest of the wedding was incredible. The reception was perfect, with dancing couples that moved to music from a live band, delicious food from Appetite's finest line, and a good time with all the people that meant the most to us.

Finally, after everything was over, we headed back home. Liam was at his grandma's house, so Izzy and I were alone. I carried her to the main bedroom as she squealed with delight. There, I stood her on her feet, helping her out of her dress.

"That was incredible," she said with a sigh. "I can't wait to get away with you tomorrow. Hawaii is going to be amazing."

I nodded, watching her step out of the dress. My cock stirred in my pants. I was so ready to consummate this marriage.

I started taking my tuxedo off. In the morning, we were taking a plane to begin our honeymoon. It was going to be wonderful. And I had so much planned for when we got back home. But right now, I wanted my wife.

I pulled her closer to me. She wore lacy white underwear and she looked breathtaking. I kissed her and ran my hands over her perfect body.

"Wait," Izzy said, "I have something for you."

"What?"

"A present," she said.

"We already exchanged wedding gifts," I said, confused.

We'd exchanged them yesterday before the rush of the wedding day.

"I know," she said. "But this is something else."

She opened her nightstand drawer and took out a small black box. It was oblong, and tied with a yellow ribbon.

I untied the ribbon and lifted the lid, looking inside. For a moment, I thought it was a pen, but it didn't look like one. It had a control window, with a plus sign in it.

"What's this?" I asked.

When I looked up at her, Izzy was beaming.

"It's a pregnancy test," she said.

I blinked. "Does this mean..."

She giggled. "Oh, Carter. I'm pregnant."

My jaw dropped, and I stared at her in stunned silence for a moment. Then it finally sank in. We were having another child.

"Oh, my God, Iz!" I cried out and grabbed her, kissing her all over. "We're having a baby!"

She laughed and let me kiss her and hug her and love her. She kissed me back, pushing her body against the length of mine, and my cock grew hard. I ran my hands down her back, and her breathing changed.

"I can't wait for our future together," I muttered as I unclasped her bra and pulled it off.

"Me either," she said and pushed her hand into my pants. I gasped when she wrapped her fingers around my length.

We stopped talking. I kissed her and touched her all over, committing every inch of her to memory. I ran my hands over her curves—her perfect hips, her delicious ass, the swell of her breasts. I kissed a trail down her abdomen and got lost in her sex. When I positioned myself over her, both of us naked, her legs fell open for me and I slid into her.

Being with her was incredible. When we were together, it felt like the rest of the world fell away and there was nothing but the two of us. She gasped and cried out softly as we came together, and I shuddered and trembled as she took me to places only she could.

We were perfect together, and we had found each other by some miracle. We had a beautiful son together, and now we were married and going to have another child.

No matter how hard I'd worked, how much money I'd earned, and how many people had learned my name, it had never been enough. Izzy was the person who made it all worth it in the end. She was the one who had shown me what it meant to love without limits, to care deeply and to live passionately. She was the one who taught me that destiny and fate and soul mates were real.

From the moment I saw her behind that counter in the café near campus, my heart had belonged to her. It had just taken me five years to figure it out.

But those five years had brought us closer to each other in one important way, because we would never take our relationship for granted. We knew what we'd lost, and we knew what we had now. That was surely the recipe for a good marriage—to never forget how lucky you were.

I was beyond fortunate to have Izzy in my life. To have her as my wife. I was so lucky to be the father to such a wonderful boy, and to have another child on the way.

"I love you, Isabelle," I whispered through our kisses and love making.

"I love you, too, Carter," she said. "And I love being your wife."

I kissed her again. I poured everything I felt into that kiss, trying to show her how much she meant to me, because words didn't come close.

And somehow, she knew. Because in her kiss, I could feel just how much she loved me, too.

If you liked this book, you'll LOVE Come Back to Me!

Ten years ago, Gavin crushed my heart.

Now the cocky prick is my boss.

I spent a decade running from my past.
Now I'm back in our small town.
There's no escape from Mr. Chiseled Abs.
When he offers me a job, I can't refuse.

I'm not one to forgive and forget.
But when he whispers my name, my insides melt.
I swore I'd never fall for Gavin again.
But here I am.
Back in the arms of the man who broke my heart.

This could be our second chance at love...
Or maybe I'm about to get burned all over again.

Start reading Come Back to Me NOW!

COME BACK TO ME: PROLOGUE
SNEAK PEEK!

JOLIE

Ten Years Ago

*T*he worst day of my life started out on such a high note.

I couldn't stop grinning as I waited for my boyfriend to pick me up for school. I was on top of the world, and with good reason.

A new world was right around the corner. High school graduation, freedom, and moving to the city.

Best of all, I'd be with the love of my life.

Little did I know, he was about to break my heart.

"Looking good, babe!" Gavin shouted through the open window of his truck.

He pulled his old Ford Bronco to the curb in front of my house, just as he did every morning. His blue eyes locked on mine, and my heart did a flip.

I waved goodbye to my mom, who watched from the doorway.

"Hi, Mrs. Adams!" Gavin called to her.

"You kids behave yourselves," she said, smiling, before she closed the front door.

"What are you all dressed up for?" he asked as I hopped in the passenger side.

Our friends Anna and Ryan were in the backseats. As always, the seat next to Gavin was reserved for me.

I shrugged. "It's our last week of high school. I guess I'm just excited."

I was wearing the dress he'd given me for my eighteenth birthday. It was a peach floral print that reached to my midcalf. It was just my style, even if it was fancier than what I usually wore to school.

I leaned toward Gavin and gave him a quick kiss. "Good morning!" I said brightly.

Gavin smiled. "Good morning yourself, gorgeous. Got another of those for me?"

"For you, baby? I happen to have an unlimited supply," I said.

Ryan made a gagging sound from the backseat. I ignored it. Leaning toward Gavin, I kissed him longer this time.

"Um, sorry to interrupt your tongue wrestling match," Anna said, "but could you two maybe be just a little less nauseating? I mean, my mom makes a great breakfast, but I'm not sure I feel like tasting it twice in one morning."

"Oh, you're just jealous because your boyfriend isn't as handsome as mine," I teased.

Anna turned to Ryan, elbowing him in the ribs. "Hey! Aren't you supposed to be offended by that remark?"

Ryan shrugged. "What can I say? I'm not so insecure in my masculinity that I won't admit it: Gavin's a damn good-looking guy. If I weren't straight, I'd date him."

"Gee, thanks for that, man," Gavin replied, glancing at

him in the rearview mirror with an amused grimace. "If I get any unsigned cards on Valentine's Day next year, I guess I'll know where they came from, huh?"

"So, what's the news from around town today?" I asked. It was a game we often played on the way to school.

"Wow, I mean, where to start?" Gavin smirked. "The mailman was pretty sure he saw a woodchuck behind his house. They called a town meeting about that one."

"And Kurt from the hardware store bought a new weed whacker," Anna chimed in with a grin. "CNN sent a camera crew to cover that."

"Don't forget about the new coat of paint that's drying on the door of the post office," Ryan said, laughing. "Thrilling stuff. I'll definitely be watching that later, if I can handle that kind of excitement."

"God, it's going to feel so good to get out of this town and live in a real place for once!" I exclaimed happily. "After this summer, it'll be Roanoke and parties and music! No more counting off the days in a place where nothing ever happens except tourist season."

"Tourist season, ha," Ryan scoffed. "Won't be missing that either. Bunch of obnoxious out-of-towners getting drunk all summer, puking in the streets, and nearly drowning in the lake. Remember that guy who fell off the charter boat last summer? Geez."

"Those people might suck, granted," Gavin reminded him, "but without them, my dad wouldn't have made nearly as much money from all his hotels."

"Yeah, that really seemed to make him happy, too," Anna said sarcastically.

A shadow passed over Gavin's face, and we all fell into an awkward silence. His father Robert's ruthless and miserly nature had been a long-running joke in our little town of

North Haven, Virginia. We had made comments like Anna's ever since we were all kids, even Gavin himself.

His dad had been the richest man in town. He'd also been the most unpopular, considered by many to be callous and greedy. He wasn't the best father to Gavin and his brothers, either.

But Gavin's parents had been killed by a drunk driver only a year before. Sometimes, it was a bit too easy for us to forget that he was still dealing with the grief.

"Hey, I'm sorry," Anna said, reaching forward and squeezing Gavin's shoulder. "That was a shitty thing for me to say."

He gave her a small smile that didn't reach his eyes. "It's okay. Really. And you're right. The fact that he's dead now doesn't mean he wasn't kind of a prick while he was alive."

I put a hand on his knee to comfort him, and he looked over at me gratefully.

"Everything's going to be okay," I told him. "Soon, we'll be off to college together, and we'll be able to put this whole place behind us and start our actual lives."

"Damn right," he said, giving me a smile. "Can't wait."

God, he was so handsome and loving and amazing. Sometimes I had a hard time believing that he was my boyfriend. How could I have been so lucky to find someone like Gavin? He'd never done anything to shake my faith in our relationship over the course of three years.

I'd found the perfect guy.

The previous month, when I had given him my virginity, he had been so gentle, so tender, so concerned with making sure I was really ready. It had been a little fumbling and awkward like most first times probably were, but it had still been amazing because it was with him.

And we had so much more of that ahead of us!

I leaned close, whispering in his ear playfully, "Soon, we

won't have to sneak around after my mom goes to sleep. We can just go to each other's dorm rooms to have sex, like normal people."

He grinned from ear to ear. "I'll have to come up with some way to let my roommate know when you're there so he doesn't walk in on us."

"There's the old hang a sock on the doorknob trick," Anna suggested helpfully.

"Yeah," Ryan snickered, "or the old hang up a sign that says We're Boning In Here, Come Back In Two Minutes trick."

"You're such an asshole." Gavin laughed.

I loved his smile. I couldn't wait to spend the rest of my life doing everything I could to make sure he did it as often as possible.

First Roanoke University, I thought happily, and then the world!

He pulled into the parking lot of North Haven High, and I jumped out of the truck. "I've got to run on ahead. I did this extra credit assignment for Ms. Maxwell, and I have to get it in to her before the bell."

"Cool, I'll catch up with you later!" Gavin called after me.

"See you soon," I said as I hurried off.

I glanced back to see him bending down to inspect some minor scratch on the body of the Bronco.

Gavin's father had hated that twenty-year-old vehicle when he'd been alive. He could never understand why his son hadn't wanted something new and sleek. But Gavin loved that old truck. He'd fixed it up and made it just as nice as anything new.

"It's a classic," he'd tell anyone who would listen.

I smiled to myself. I could hardly wait for our life together to begin.

As I bounded up the front steps of the school, I started to

feel weird, like everyone spoke in a whisper as soon as I'd gotten close.

I looked around.

Everyone was staring at me. Some of them appeared to be horrified, a few of them were trying to stifle laughter, but all of their eyes were on me. They all knew something I didn't.

Dread filled my chest. I didn't know what was waiting for me on the other side of that door, but something inside me was too afraid to take another step. It wanted me to turn and run away as fast as I could, to make up any excuse—that I was suddenly sick or that I had a family emergency. Anything to get away from that awful sea of eyes blinking at me.

Instead, I summoned all my courage, put my hand on the metal bar of the door, and pulled it open.

The walls and lockers were all heavily papered with copies of the same black and white photograph. Several faculty members were yanking them down by the fistful as quickly as possible, while the students just stared at them.

And at me.

"Jolie!" Ms. Maxwell hurried down the hall toward me, dropping an armload of the photos into a nearby trash can. She had a worried expression on her face. "Jolie, no, don't come in yet! Wait outside, please! Everything's all right, but just wait."

I looked at the photo on those pages. The picture was so surreal to me, so unbelievable, that it took my mind a few seconds to process it.

When I finally did—when I understood what I was looking at—I felt my entire world shatter, like a crystal ornament dropped on the floor.

Then, I did turn and run. As fast as my legs could carry me.

In some ways, I wasn't sure I ever stopped.

Grab your copy of Come Back to Me here!

COME BACK TO ME: CHAPTER 1
SNEAK PEEK!

GAVIN

*M*adison's skirt was short.

Again.

It was even shorter than it had been the previous day, which I hadn't realized was possible since that one was so high that it had seemed like little more than a thick belt around her waist.

This one was practically a ribbon.

She wanted me to notice, and of course I did. But from the way she bent over the desk to put paperwork in front of me—the sensual smiles she gave me and the astonishingly obvious come-hither look in her eyes whenever they met mine—I knew that she also wanted a lot more than that.

And what she wanted would make things complicated. Which I didn't need.

So I did my best to keep my eyes on my desk. I didn't want to encourage her. I figured if I stuck to my guns long enough, she'd get bored and find someone else to wiggle those hips at.

Kevin Banks sat across from me. His eyes were shamelessly locked on her curves. He waited for her to be out of earshot then let out a low whistle. "Oh man, please tell me you're getting a slice of that on a regular basis."

"Nope." I made a show of studying the blueprints for what would be my newest—and most luxurious—hotel.

"You're kidding!" he balked. "Why the hell not? Didn't you see the way she was looking at you? She clearly wants you!"

I sighed, putting the blueprints aside. "Yes. But Madison wants the whole silly scenario. She wants me to ask her to work late, suggest we order in dinner, share some jokes. And somewhere along the way, it all turns into rolling around on the floor among the manila folders and contracts."

"So?" Kevin chuckled. "What's the problem with that?"

"The problem is, I've fallen for it before. And I'm sick of having to hire a new assistant every few months. Because after the sex, they want relationships."

"Well, if you don't want her, I'll take her."

"You have my blessing to give it a shot," I said, looking at the blueprints again. "But—no offense—I don't think you're Madison's type."

Kevin's eyes wandered down to his beer belly and a hand fluttered over his balding scalp. He cleared his throat.

"Now, if you don't mind," I said. "I'd like to get back to finalizing the location of the new hotel."

Kevin raised an eyebrow. "What's to finalize? The location is obvious. You want it on Lake Moore, and the perfect lot for the hotel is available on the west side of it. A bit pricey, sure, but not beyond your means, especially given how much you'll make when it opens. That spot will give your guests the best view of the lake and put them close enough to the water for you to set them up with water taxi tours, charter fishing, the whole shebang."

"I want the hotel on the east side of the lake," I said flatly.

"It doesn't make sense, though. The west side has the better view," Kevin protested.

He was right about the lake views of the western lot. But it wasn't just the lake that brought tourists. North Haven was set in a picturesque valley of the Blue Ridge Mountains of southern Virginia. The views were stunning every way a person looked. Not to mention the charm that the town had to offer. It was why my business tycoon father had picked North Haven to develop before I was born.

"You told me all that already," I reminded him. "And I told you, find another spot."

Kevin blinked at me, confused. "Okay, well, maybe if I knew why you object to building on that lot, I'd be in a better position to provide you with alternatives."

I knew full well that Kevin didn't give a shit about providing me with alternatives. He was just damn nosy, like the rest of the busybodies in North Haven. In a town that size, none of the locals ever minded their own business. During the off season, when the tourists weren't around to raise hell, gossip was the only real source of entertainment for most of the people who lived there year-round.

Still, I supposed I had to tell him, if that was what it took for him to drop the subject and look for a different location.

"Teresa Adams lives next to that lot," I said. "It would make her unhappy."

"Yeah, no shit," Kevin snorted. "But your hotel will make all the locals unhappy. They already think your resorts are taking up too much lakefront space. Why should she be any different?"

He had a point. I usually didn't care about who I disturbed by putting my buildings where I did. My father hadn't become a business mogul by worrying about every little guy he came across. Cole Enterprises was still thriving, even after he was gone. And that was because I was willing to do just about anything to keep it going.

But this property was different.

I stood up and turned to look out the window.

When this had been Dad's office, it had been all expensive woods—mahogany desk and stately chairs. Even wooden pens, which had been bizarre to me.

When he'd actually spent time with me during his life, Dad had always told me I needed to be more styled and put together with everything from my first beat-up truck to my clothes. I'd gotten rid of the truck in college, and I'd cleaned up my look well before business school.

And a few years ago, when I'd taken over the business from the trustees that had managed it after my parents' death, I'd had the office redone in sleek lines. All grays, blacks, and leathers. But its modern, pristine look made it uncomfortable. I often found myself restless.

"Kevin, you're the best commercial building contractor in three counties. You've built my last two hotels for me. I want you to build this one, and hopefully a whole bunch more down the line. But in order for that to happen, I suggest you propose a different location."

"Or what?" he laughed. "You'll hire Donald Markinson and his crew of drunks? Or hey, I'm sure you could get a good estimate from Phil Baxter. This past year, I heard that he actually had four of his projects up to code out of ten."

I spun around and eyed him.

He raised his hands defensively. "Come on, Gavin, there's no need to play hardball. I'm just trying to help! I need to know what you're thinking so I can do that. I mean, what if there's something about the next lot I ask you to consider that would somehow piss her off too?"

I rolled my eyes. "Fine. If you must know, it would seriously lower the value of Teresa Adams's house. She's getting older, and she might decide to sell it someday if she needs the money. And if she does, she should be able to get as much as possible for it. Besides, putting a six-story hotel there would block her view of the lake. That view always meant a lot to her."

Kevin tilted his head. "Wow. Okay. How do you know so much about Mrs. Adams?" Before I could answer, he snapped his fingers, remembering. "Oh, that's right! Didn't I once hear that you used to date her daughter in high school? What was her name again? Janie? Julie?"

"Jolie."

Just uttering the name out loud made me feel like I had a bone stuck in my throat. All the old memories were coming back, whistling through the air, and burying themselves deep in my heart like daggers.

"So, hang on. Is that what this thing with the Adams lady is about?" Kevin demanded. "Are you still sweet on this Jolie chick after all these years? Yikes, man. I guess that would also explain why you aren't hopping all over Madison like a bunny in springtime, huh? I mean, ten years, that's a hell of a long time to still be carrying a torch."

I gritted my teeth. What could I say to him? That I had never lived down the guilt of how I had hurt her? That no matter how many years went by, all it took was the sudden memory of her humiliation—the look that twisted her face to tears as she ran out of the school and pushed past me—to make me brood for days? Ten years, and the pain was still as sharp as it had been on the day it happened.

If I had known that those kisses in the car would be the last ones we'd ever have, I wouldn't have gone to classes that day. I'd have dropped off Anna and Ryan and spent the whole rest of the day with her. I'd have tried to somehow make those hours last forever.

But since Jolie had left town after graduation—angrily vowing never to speak to me again—I figured trying to look out for her mother's best interests was the very least I could do.

If that meant making sure her property value didn't get destroyed, so be it.

She'd been like a second mother to me when my world fell apart after my parents' deaths. She deserved any help I could give her.

Madison poked her head in, her blonde hair framing the look of concern on her face. "Sorry, I don't mean to interrupt, but did I hear you guys talking about Teresa Adams?"

"No need to apologize, darling. You can interrupt me anytime!" Kevin said with a lascivious wink. I was half surprised he didn't pat his lap and offer her a seat there. "And yes, as a matter of fact, we were discussing Mrs. Adams. What about her?"

"Well, I see her at the grocery store sometimes, and whenever we've chatted, she's been really nice," Madison said, her mouth a fretful little red O as she sat on the couch. "And I just think it's really sad, you know? What she's been going through."

"What? Dealing with the prospect of seeing a luxury hotel whenever she looks out the window?" Kevin grunted derisively. "Hardly a tragedy, wouldn't you say? More of a mild inconvenience, when you come right down to it."

"Oh no." Her eyes widened. "You didn't hear what happened?"

"I know that her husband left her," I answered, trying to keep my tone neutral.

Kevin chortled. "Wow, you really have been keeping tabs on this lady, haven't you, buddy?"

"But that was almost a year ago," I went on, ignoring his comment. "Surely she's recovered from that since then."

"No, not that," Madison replied, wincing. "She got diagnosed with breast cancer. And I heard it was pretty bad."

I sat back in my chair, feeling all the air leave my lungs at once. "No, Madison. I hadn't heard that."

I cleared my throat and then stood up and crossed to the door.

"We're done here, Kevin. Find me a different lot."

I opened the door and waited as Kevin blinked then nodded.

"Whatever you say, Gavin," he said. He scampered to his feet and walked out the door.

Madison lounged on the couch and gave me a sly smile.

"Bye, Madison," I said as I jerked my head toward the door. She dropped the seductive look abruptly before hurrying out the office.

I returned to the window and sighed.

I wondered when Jolie had heard this news and how she had taken it. She must have been devastated. I wanted to look up her phone number, to call her, to make sure she was all right.

Except I knew that hearing from me would probably just make her feel worse.

No, the best thing I could do for her at that point was make sure she never had to see me—or even think about me —ever again.

No matter how difficult that prospect was for me.

As hard as I'd tried to forget her over the past ten years, Jolie's memory was seared in my mind.

The first, and only, girl I'd ever loved.

Grab your copy of Come Back to Me NOW!

Printed in Great Britain
by Amazon

78499198R00144